HIGH COUNTRY HERO

BROTHERHOOD PROTECTORS COLORADO
BOOK TWELVE

ELLE JAMES

TWISTED PAGE INC

HIGH COUNTRY HERO

BROTHERHOOD PROTECTORS COLORADO
BOOK #12

New York Times & USA Today
Bestselling Author

ELLE JAMES

© 2023 Twisted Page Inc. All rights reserved.

ISBN EBOOK: 978-1-62695-535-6

ISBN PRINT: 978-1-62695-533-2

A big thank you to my parents who taught me the value of hard work, determination and family love. I miss you both so much.
Elle James

AUTHOR'S NOTE

Enjoy other military romance books by Elle James

Brotherhood Protectors Colorado
SEAL Salvation (#1)
Rocky Mountain Rescue (#2)
Ranger Redemption (#3)
Tactical Takeover (#4)
Colorado Conspiracy (#5)
Rocky Mountain Madness (#6)
Free Fall (#7)
Colorado Cold Case (#8)
Fool's Folly (#9)
Colorado Free Rein (#10)
Rocky Mountain Venom (#11)
High Country Hero (#12)

Visit ellejames.com for more titles and release dates
Join her newsletter at
https://ellejames.com/contact/

CHAPTER 1

"In position," Chief Special Operator Enrico "Rico" Cortez was last to report after he and Roberto "Bert" Ramirez achieved the forward-most position on the edge of the target compound. They'd cover for the others as they moved forward.

"Task Force Smash-n-Grab, move out," Lieutenant Metcalf's order came through Rico's headset.

The US Navy SEAL team slipped through the night, closing in on the ISIS-held location where three US Army Forward Surgical Team members had been taken after capture.

The SEAL team's mission: extract the surgeon, anesthetist and a nurse. Two males and one female. ISIS had ambushed the team en route to perform humanitarian work in a recently bombed village in northwestern Syria. An informant had indicated they'd targeted the FST to bring them to one of their leaders who'd been injured in a raid against Syrian Democratic Forces.

From what the informant had learned, the ISIS leader, Khalid Sukkar, hadn't made it through the surgery, and the FST members were being tortured and held in horrific conditions.

The sooner the SEAL team freed them, the better, before there was nothing left to liberate.

This ISIS faction, under the new leadership of Sukkar's second in command, wasn't known for their mercy. If anything, Sukkar's replacement was even more violent than his predecessor.

Rico would be surprised if the FST members were still alive. If they were, they'd be in bad shape. The team would likely have to carry them out. And if they took out every one of the ISIS bastards in the process... Good. Under International Law, Humanitarian Law, Geneva Convention and just common sense and honor, combatants didn't fuck with medical personnel.

From the informant's report, the FST members had been royally fucked with.

"Let's get 'em," the lieutenant said.

The team moved into the compound, picking their way through the rubble of bombed-out structures to the semi-intact buildings at the center of what had once been a thriving village perched on a hillside.

As described by the informant, the building at the

center of the village was surrounded by a six-foot-tall wall with a one-story structure sprawled inside the center.

The hairs on the back of Rico's neck stiffened. "Where are all the guards?"

"I thought this was an ISIS stronghold," Patch said. "Think they've moved out?"

"That or dug into the hillside," LT suggested.

"Got a bogey half-asleep on the east corner rooftop," Bert's voice came through Rico's headset.

Rico glanced up at the spot. A man dressed all in black with a black turban wrapped around his head held an AK-47 rifle. He swayed and jerked as if falling in and out of sleep while standing.

"Got him in my sights," whispered the team's sniper, TJ Murphy.

A muted report of the sniper's rifle suppressor sounded from the corner of a building.

The man swaying on the rooftop slumped over and dropped out of sight on the roof.

Rico's muscles tensed.

"Rico, Bert, take point," LT ordered.

"Roger," Rico and Bert replied as one.

With the team covering, Rico and Bert approached the east wall.

Bert leaned his submachine gun against the wall, bent and cupped his hands.

Rico slung his rifle over his shoulder, stepped into his buddy's palms and pulled himself up onto the

ELLE JAMES

wall. Flattening his body against the top, he peered into the shadows.

An eerie silence greeted him. Nothing moved in the shadows. He didn't like it. A single guard on the roof but none around the building didn't bode well for what they might find inside. "Other than the guard on the roof, this place appears to be abandoned," he whispered into his mic.

"Move in," LT ordered.

Rico reached a hand down to Bert.

The man grasped it and walked up the wall until he could throw his arms over the top and pull himself up.

The team approached the wall. One by one, they scaled it and dropped to the other side.

They spread out, surrounding the exterior of the structure.

Rico and Bert found the front entrance.

Standing to the side of the door, Rico tried to turn the knob.

Locked.

He pulled out the small crowbar affixed to the back of his armor-plated vest, inserted it between the door and the frame and gave it a sharp jolt. The door opened, swinging inward.

Rico nodded to Bert in the darkness. "Cover."

"I've got your six," Bert said. "Go."

Rico, crouching low, his rifle held out in front of

him, ducked through the door and darted to the right.

Again, nothing moved.

Wooden crates lined the walls, their lids removed, the packaging materials scattered across the floor in front of them.

The writing on the sides of the crates was in Russian. Based on the length and width of the boxes, Rico would bet the contents had been AK-47 rifles or the dreaded flame throwers this faction liked to employ against their enemies and villages full of women and children. They were brutal, and their methods of torture inhumane.

Once inside the building, the team went from room to room.

Rico and Bert led the effort, arriving at the very back of the building, having found no people and no signs of habitation other than the crates, dusty piles of trash and remnants of tattered rugs in each room.

But people had been here. Recently. The dust on the floor leading down a long hallway had been disturbed with enough feet to obliterate individual footprints, all ending at a pile of tattered rugs lying in a bunch near the far corner of the last room.

Rico nudged the pile with the barrel of his rifle. The rugs didn't move far, the base of the pile seeming stuck to the floor.

Bert and Rico pulled the top layers of the rugs

away, revealing the lower remnants were nailed to a wood trap door.

"It's a goddamn spider hole," Bert said softly.

A shiver of apprehension rippled across Rico's skin and up the back of his neck.

The team gathered in the room, shining flashlights at the spider hole.

Rico nodded toward Bert.

"I got your back," Bert said.

As Rico reached for the corner of the wood, the door lurched upward and a bearded man's head emerged, wrapped in a black turban. He held a flashlight in his hand, shining it into the room.

When he spotted the men standing around the room, his eyes widened.

Rico reacted instinctively, slamming the butt of his rifle into the man's face as hard as he could.

He fell backward into the hole, and the trap door dropped closed.

Bert yanked it open. Rico dropped down into the hole, landing on the man he'd hit. In the glow from the flashlight the man had dropped, Rico yanked out his knife and quickly dispatched the man to keep him from raising the alarm.

Rico dragged the man out of the way. He pointed his rifle with the flashlight attached to the barrel down a dark tunnel carved out of the side of the hill. Once Bert had lowered himself into the spider hole, Rico set off.

Other members of the team entered the tunnel behind them.

Rico hunkered low to keep from scraping his helmet against the narrow, earthen ceiling and moved quickly and silently until the tunnel opened into a larger room.

Chains hung from the ceiling, sticks leaned against the wall, and plastic bags lay in one corner next to a couple of old tires. A barrel full of rancid water stood in another corner, and dark patches stained the floor. The room smelled of sweat, urine, feces and decay.

Bile rose in Rico's throat. This room he'd entered had to be the torture room. He didn't hold out much hope of finding the FST members alive. If they were alive, they'd be in terrible shape.

Two tunnels branched off from the torture room. Rico, Bert, TJ and Skeeter entered the left tunnel. Four others took the right branch.

Several yards into the tunnel, Rico found a metal door with a locking lever on the outside.

Bert pointed his rifle at the door as Rico lifted the latch and swung the door open. The flashlight attached to the barrel of Bert's weapon swept into the tight room.

At first, Rico thought the room was empty until Bert's light reached the corner to his right, where a lump of what appeared to be dirt stirred, and a weak groan rose out of the dirt.

Rico entered the room as a naked man, covered in dried blood and filth, lifted his head and stared at them with dull eyes.

As Rico approached, he shrank back against the wall.

"Colonel Estep?" Rico whispered.

The man shook his head and wrapped his arms around his legs.

"Captain Monahan?" Rico crouched beside him.

The prisoner nodded, his eyes rounding.

"We're here to get you out."

"Sweet Jesus," he croaked.

Rico slid the man's arm around his neck and helped him to his feet.

The man moaned and slumped to the ground.

"His feet are bleeding." TJ entered the room. "We'll carry him. Look for the others." TJ and Skeeter lifted the man between them and carried him out of the cell and down the tunnel.

Rico and Bert moved further down the tunnel to the next door and lifted the latch. Inside, they found a man lying on the floor, his arms secured behind his back with a leather strap. Shirtless, his back was crisscrossed with raw slashes as if he'd been beaten with a whip or sticks. He stirred when Rico and Bert entered the room.

"No more. Please," he murmured.

Rico squatted beside him. "Colonel Estep?"

The man groaned. "Yes."

"We're here to get you out," Rico said.

The colonel's shoulders shook with silent sobs.

"Can you walk?" Rico asked as he cut through the leather strap, freeing the man's wrists.

Colonel Estep nodded.

Rico helped him to his feet. The man swayed and fell against the wall. He straightened himself. "Monahan and Layne?" he asked, his voice hoarse."

"We found Monahan. He's being evacuated."

"Layne?"

"Not yet. Bert will help you out."

The colonel shook his head and steadied himself with a hand on the wall. "Not leaving without Layne."

Rico helped the man out of the cell and left him with Bert. He went further into the tunnel, reaching the end without finding another door.

As he turned to retrace his steps, the floor beneath him made a hollow sound. He shined the light on his rifle at the ground to discover a trap door.

He laid his rifle on the ground, shining the light over the ground. With his fingers, he traced the edge of a two-foot square of sheet metal and lifted it off a hole in the ground.

Unlike the spider hole leading into the tunnel, this hole was the width of an oil barrel and dark.

Rico lifted his rifle and pointed it into the hole. A pair of blue eyes blinked up at him from a dark face.

"Captain Layne?" he asked.

A quick sob sounded. The head ducked down, the eyes disappearing.

"It's okay," he said softly. "I'm not going to hurt you. Let me help you out of there."

The head lifted, and the eyes blinked up at him, swimming in tears.

He laid his weapon down again. The light shining over the top of the hole cast the occupant inside in darkness.

Rico reached down. "Can you take my hand?"

"No," a gravelly voice sounded.

He laid on his belly and reached deeper into the darkness, his hands skimming over a shorn head and lower to narrow shoulders. His hands gripped beneath the arms, and he lifted, scooting backward as he did until the person at the bottom of the hole was bent over the top edge.

He let go to straighten into a kneeling position to get a better grip.

The prisoner slipped backward over the edge.

Rico grabbed beneath an arm and fell backward onto the ground, taking the prisoner with him.

His arm encircled a naked female body and steadied her. He'd found the nurse, Captain Layne.

"Are you okay?" he asked.

In the faint glow of the flashlight on his rifle, he stared up into eyes so light blue they stood out in a filthy, dirty face. Her hair had been shaved from her head, and every inch of her body was covered in what smelled like sewage.

Rico rolled her off him gently, her body coming to rest on her side. She winced and tried to pull her knees up to her chest, whimpering.

Pulling his knife from its sheath, Rico cut the bindings from her wrists.

She moved slowly, her face pinched in pain as she wrapped her arms over her breasts.

Rico shed his vest with the armored plates and removed his uniform jacket.

He helped her into a sitting position and gently wrapped her in the jacket, noting the slashes across her back, the oozing sores on her inner thighs and her bloody feet. What had this woman endured?

God, he didn't want to know. His job was to get her out. The sooner, the better.

Gunfire echoed in the tunnel.

"The hornets' nest is officially stirred," the LT's voice sounded. "Get out while we hold them."

"You got the girl, Rico?" Bert's voice sounded in his ear.

"Got her," Rico responded.

"Targets acquired," Bert reported. "Heading out."

Rico pushed to his feet. He didn't have time to slip back into the vest, which would only weigh him down further. He had to get the woman out.

Now.

He pulled the flashlight off the barrel, slung his rifle over his shoulder and lifted the nurse into his arms. She was as small and light as a child and painfully thin. "Hang on. We're making a run for it." With the flashlight pointing forward, he headed back the way he'd come, soon catching up to Bert and Colonel Estep, moving slowly through the torture chamber.

"TJ and Skeeter got Monahan out," Bert said. "The rest of the team is holding the bogeys at bay."

"We have incoming up here," Patch, the external team leader, said in Rico's ear. "Two truckloads of militants heading our way. We'll hold them back, but you have to get out now. It's about to get hot."

Gunfire sounded in the other tunnel.

"We're heading for the exit point," the LT's voice sounded in Rico's ear.

"Go!" Bert said. "Doc, follow them. I'll cover the rear."

Rico ran through the torture room.

Layne pressed her dirty face into his shirt, her arm around his neck, barely able to hold on.

When they reached the spider hole, TJ was there. He reached down, grasped Layne's arms and drew her through the narrow hole.

Rico pulled himself up and out, then turned to help the colonel to the surface. Though the man was thin and weak from starvation, he was heavier than Layne. Rico strained to pull the colonel up and out of the hole.

Bert was next, followed by three more members of their team, each popping out one at a time.

"Fire in the hole," the lieutenant cried. He fired his rifle, pulled himself out of the spider hole, slammed the trapdoor down and covered his ears just in time.

An explosion lifted the trap door several inches into the air. As it landed, the lieutenant scrambled to his feet.

TJ grabbed Monahan's arm and dragged him up and over his shoulder in a fireman's carry. He took off at a dead run through the hallway of the building.

The lieutenant looped the colonel's arm over his shoulder and followed TJ, moving as fast as he could with the colonel leaning heavily against him.

Rico gathered the nurse in his arms and ran, Bert bringing up the rear.

When they emerged into the open, gunfire pierced the previously silent night.

"Over here!" Skeeter called from the wall where they'd entered the compound. He'd dragged a wooden crate out of the building and placed it against the wall.

TJ ran for the crate with Monahan over his back. Skeeter leaped onto the wall; TJ handed Monahan up to him and climbed up and over, dropping down on the other side.

Skeeter eased Monahan down on the other side and slid over the wall after him.

The lieutenant half-ran, half-dragged the colonel

to the crate. The three men who'd been with him in the other tunnel ran ahead and helped get the colonel over the wall.

Rico handed Layne into the hands of the men helping them over the wall and pulled himself up and over in time to receive the nurse on the other side.

He waited long enough to ensure Bert made it over with the other members of the team who'd breached the wall with them. Once they were all on the other side, he ran with Layne clutched close to his chest, Bert covering the rear.

The other members of the team, who'd remained outside the walled compound and had held down the incoming truckloads of combatants, eased back through the village streets, quickly catching up to Bert.

Their goal was to make it to the hillside just outside the village, where Black Hawk helicopters would pick them up and ferry them back to their Forward Operating Base. A medical team waited there to stabilize and accompany the FST members to a higher level of medical support in Germany. Once they could withstand a longer flight, they'd be transported to the States to recover.

They just had to get them on that Black Hawk and out of range of ISIS anti-aircraft weapons.

Rico kept moving forward, following the others, carrying Layne. The colonel slowed the lieutenant down to the point that Metcalf stopped and tossed the doc over his shoulder in a fireman carry. He was able to move faster, even weighed down by the man. Weaving through the rubble and destroyed portions of the village, the team finally emerged on the edge of the town and raced out into the open.

Bert and three other team members hung back, laying down cover fire to keep the ISIS combatants from advancing on the guys carrying the injured Forward Surgical Team members.

Skeeter called in the Black Hawks.

Two helicopters swooped in. One aimed for the hillside, the other flew closer to the village and unloaded fifty-caliber gunfire in front of the line of SEALs holding back ISIS gunmen.

TJ reached the chopper first and handed off Monahan to the flight medics aboard, then jumped.

Rico felt something hit the back of his left calf, making him stumble. He fell to his knees, still holding Layne in his arms. After regaining his balance, Rico lurched to his feet and limped forward, picking up speed despite the pain in his left calf.

"Fuck!" Bert said. "Some of those bastards got through further south of our position. Heading that way."

"Negative, Bert," the lieutenant said into Rico's headset. "Pull back and head for the extraction point."

An explosion sounded behind Rico. He turned to

see a cloud of dust and debris blurring his view of the village.

"Bert." Rico slowed to a halt.

"I'm hit," Bert called out. "Keep going. I'll hold them off. Get those people out."

Rico shook his head. "We're not leaving without you."

"You have to. There are too many of them. If you don't get out now, you might not make it out. Get them out."

"Move, Rico. Get Layne on that chopper," Lt. Metcalf ordered.

Rico leaned forward, limping heavily. He gritted his teeth and powered ahead, refusing to let the pain in his leg or his draining strength stop him. If he could get the woman to the chopper, he could turn around and go back for Bert.

As he reached the helicopter, hands reached for Captain Layne, pulling her up into the aircraft.

When Rico spun to head back for Bert, the dust was settling where the explosion had occurred. Dark silhouettes emerged from between the buildings on the edge of the village. A flash of flame burst through the air.

"They have flame throwers," a voice said into Rico's ear.

"Get out of here!" Bert cried as a burst of machine gun fire forced the ISIS combatants to drop to the ground.

All the men but Bert had made it back to the chopper.

When Bert's gunfire ceased, the black silhouettes rose and moved forward again, the flame thrower belching a stream of fire, sweeping back and forth across the ground.

Bert's machine gun went off.

The man holding the flame thrower crumpled to the ground, dropping the weapon.

Another man picked it up and kept moving forward.

Another burst of gunfire sounded from Bert's weapon.

Rico lunged away from the Black Hawk, half-running, half-limping toward Bert.

The gunfire didn't last long, cutting off suddenly.

The black silhouettes rushed forward, the flame lashing out.

"Well, damn," Bert said. "My gun's jammed. Why the hell haven't you left yet? Get out of here. Tell my wife and kids I love them. You know I love you guys," he said.

The flame swept across the ground, scorching brush and grass.

"Out here," Bert said. A single shot sounded.

"Bert," Rico cried. "Bert!"

He didn't answer.

The flame finally caught a huddled figure on the ground, lighting it up in the night.

"No!" Rico staggered forward. In his heart, he knew. Bert was gone. But he couldn't leave him behind.

The second helicopter had circled around and swept in, laying down fire on the ISIS combatants.

Two of Rico's teammates grabbed his arms and dragged him back to the helicopter. Other hands reached down and pulled him up into the aircraft as the last two men dove on board.

Even as the helicopter rose from the ground, Rico fought to get out. Go back. Bring Bert home. His teammates forced him into a seat and buckled the harness around him.

A truckload of ISIS burst from the edge of the village, ground to a halt and unloaded the men on board. One of the men pulled out a long, narrow tube and lifted it to his shoulder.

By then, the helicopter was well up in the sky, heading over the top of the ridge.

The other chopper turned and fired a rocket at the truck. But not before the ISIS rocket left the hand-held launcher.

The truck exploded.

"Incoming!" Lieutenant Metcalf yelled.

Rico closed his eyes, fully expecting the rocket to slam into the side of the Black Hawk.

The chopper dove behind the hill. The rocket slammed into the ridge, the force of the explosion rocking them.

The pilot struggled for control, steadied the aircraft and picked up speed, leaving ISIS, the village and Bert behind.

Rico stared out at the night, his heart heavy and feeling sick to his stomach. His best friend was gone. He'd known that flame would reach him soon, and he'd chosen to go out on his own terms. He would not have suffered. He'd sacrificed himself to save his team.

He was a hero.

But what good was a dead hero?

Rico dragged his gaze back to the interior of the helicopter. They'd accomplished their mission, extracting the three members of the FST.

All three lay across the helicopter floor, the flight medic and their team medic working over them to establish IVs. Monahan was already hooked up. Though unconscious, he was breathing. He'd probably passed out while being carried from the village. Captain Layne lay at Rico's feet, staring up at him with those incredibly blue eyes. She reached up a dirty hand.

He took the hand and held it all the way to the FOB. When they landed, she refused to let go, her last bit of strength channeled into her hand, holding him.

Rico carried her out of the helicopter, almost collapsing when he put weight on his injured leg.

When others tried to take her from him, he held

on, carrying her to the stretcher. Only then did he release his hold.

She grabbed his T-shirt and pulled him close. "Thank you," she said, her voice nothing more than gravel and air. "You're my hero."

He shook his head. He wanted to say that he wasn't a hero. The hero was Robert Ramirez, who'd stayed back to cover for them. The man who'd chosen a bullet over flames as his ticket out of hell, leaving the world on his own terms.

Before Rico could say anything, two medics carried the nurse away, loaded her into an ambulance and drove her to the field hospital.

"Dude," TJ came up beside him. "You're bleeding."

"It's nothing," Rico said, his tone flat, his heart flat-lining.

"The hell it is." Lieutenant Metcalf called out, "Medic!"

"I'm fine," Rico ground out. "We need to go back for Bert."

The lieutenant laid a hand on Rico's shoulder. "Another team is already in the air, halfway there. They'll bring him back."

What was left of him. If ISIS didn't drag his charred remains through the streets.

Rico's stomach lurched. He staggered away from the others and lost the contents of his belly.

When he straightened, a medic stood beside him.

"Come with me, sir. We need to take care of that wound."

Rico didn't want to take care of his wound. Compared to what had happened to Bert, the bullet in his leg was nothing. The pain served as a reminder of what he'd lost and what he hadn't done to save his friend.

"You'll go with the medic," Metcalf said. "That's an order." He stood in front of Rico. "There was nothing any of us could do. Bert was too close. You had a job to do. You saved a life."

"And we lost a life."

"You'd have done the same thing had you been Bert and expected Bert to get that woman to safety."

"He should've been carrying her. I should've been the one left behind."

Metcalf shook his head. "He had the machine gun. It was his job, and he did it." The lieutenant tipped his head. "Go. Let them patch you up. If you die of infection, Bert's sacrifice would be in vain. You saved a life today."

"Damn it!" Rico slammed his fist into his palm. "Bert's gone. Is it right to save one life at the cost of another?"

"You saw what condition they were in. Bert wasn't tortured. He didn't suffer. Had we left those three where they were, they would've continued to suffer. They didn't have the option Bert had. You helped save them from a fate much worse."

"Yeah. Tell it to Bert's wife and kids," Rico said. "Fine. I'll get my leg patched. I'll live to fight another goddamn day."

Bert wouldn't. Rico's wingman. The guy he'd been with since BUD/S was no more.

Nothing would ever be the same.

CHAPTER 2

"THANKS FOR COMING OUT TO HELP." RJ Tate set three full beer mugs on the tray and pushed it across the bar toward Laurel. "We're always slammed when the rodeo's in town."

Laurel hefted the heavy tray and smiled. "You know I love being out here with you and Gunny. I owe you so much for loaning me the money to expand the shop."

RJ snorted as she filled another mug full of beer. "You don't owe us anything. You've paid back the loan and are doing great with your florist business. The point is, you're family. Family takes care of each other."

"Yes, we're family. I'd do anything for you and Gunny." With a grin, Laurel turned to take the tray to the table of rowdy cowboys, laughing about their day

23

at the rodeo. Over her shoulder, she called out, "I'm going to make you a special flower arrangement, RJ."

"Save the flowers for paying customers," RJ yelled over the din. "Flowers remind me too much of funerals."

Laurel nodded without turning back.

"Sorry," RJ called. "Forgot for a moment."

"No worries," Laurel swallowed hard on the lump in her throat and kept moving forward. Looking back never did her any good. Easier to focus on others, like her friend, RJ.

Having lost her mother at a young age, RJ had been raised by her Marine father. A tomboy, more at home on Lost Valley Ranch, wearing jeans and boots than at a social event in a dress, RJ was female through and through. Beneath her gruff exterior, she had a heart of gold and loved fiercely.

Laurel was so glad she'd found her match in Navy SEAL Jake Cogburn, the head of the Colorado regional office of Brotherhood Protectors.

Jake had saved RJ's life, and she'd saved him from the self-destructive track he'd been on before taking his position with the protection agency founded by another Navy SEAL, Hank Patterson.

The agency meant so much to the men they employed—men who'd served in special forces who'd left the Army, Navy, Marines and Air Force highly trained in combat and at a loss with how those skills could be used in the civilian sector. Many of the men employed suffered with PTSD and struggled to fit into their new lives.

Laurel understood PTSD. She still had nightmares from when she'd been captured and tortured by ISIS. She didn't remember much from her time in captivity and was glad of it. The external scars were enough of a reminder of that time. Her nightmares tried to bring those memories back. She often woke drenched in sweat and tears. She hated tight, dark places and preferred to be surrounded by sunlight and the beautiful colors abundant in her flower shop, Laurel's Florals, in Fool's Gold, her hometown town, nestled in the Rocky Mountains.

Laurel carried the tray of beer to the table and served the men with a smile. Life was short. She chose to be happy rather than relive the terror of her captivity and nightmares.

Her brother, Devin, hurried to a table a group of cowboys had just vacated and loaded empty drinks and plates into a tub and then wiped the table clean with a spray disinfectant and a clean rag.

"Hey, Dev," she said, "where's Mallory?"

"She's helping at the rodeo. She competes tomorrow. Otherwise, she'd be here tonight."

"She'll do well," Laurel said.

"She should," Devin said. "She's been practicing with Jazz since the last rodeo."

Laurel smiled. "Now that you two are together,

she's much more focused. And happy. You're both happy. It does my heart good."

He straightened with a grin. "We are. Crazy, stupid happy." His brow dipped low. "What about you?"

She blinked at him. "Me? I'm fine."

"Even with the reunion and memorial with your team from Syria?" he asked, his concerned gaze pinning hers.

She nodded. "I look forward to seeing Colonel Estep." She gave him a quick smile. "I should just call him Dr. Estep. He got out of the Army after Syria."

"I was sorry to hear about Captain Monahan," Devin said. "I worry about you."

Laurel shook her head. "Don't. I'm home with family and friends. I have a thriving business. I'm happy. Monahan came out of Syria a lot worse off than Dr. Estep or me. He suffered terribly."

"All three of you did," Devin said, his jaw tight. "Those bastards…"

"It's in the past. I prefer that it stays there," she said.

"Are you sure this reunion and memorial won't bring it all back?"

Laurel drew in a deep breath and let it out. "It will be good to see Dr. Estep and the others we deployed with. It might just be the event that gives us the chance to let go of what happened."

"Are you still having nightmares?" He studied her closely.

The nightmares were very much a part of her. She'd hoped, with time, they'd fade. When they hadn't, she'd learned to live with them.

Her brother's brow dipped lower. "You are still having them. You know you can move in with us. Mal would love to have you close."

Laurel shook her head. "No way. I'd be a third wheel in your lovefest. I'm content in my apartment over the shop. I have a great security system, and I'm thinking of getting a dog."

"Mal and I discussed this. We would love you to live with us. Especially after what happened with Alan Croft, aka Trent Ryan."

She squared her shoulders. "I'm over that. Alan Croft is behind bars and can't hurt me or Mallory ever again."

"Are you still seeing that therapist at the VA?" Devin asked.

Laurel nodded. "For what it's worth. I don't really need it. I'm happy, healthy and loving life."

Her brother's frown remained. "And you've been through more than most people can handle without cracking."

"If I wanted to live around people, I'd move in with RJ and Gunny in the lodge. I would not mess up a good thing between you and Mallory by intruding on young love."

"We have a new Brotherhood Protector as of today. He took the last available room in the lodge until the rodeo is over. Staying at the lodge might not be an option. Besides, the ranch house is just as much yours as it is mine. It's your home. We grew up there."

Laurel sighed. "Now, it's yours and Mal's. I have a lovely apartment above my shop. I'm comfortable and happy," she insisted.

"Miss Laurel," a cowboy called out from a table full of rabble-rousers.

"I'm fine, Devin," she said. "I came out tonight to help." And to get away from her thoughts of Monahan's suicide. She needed to keep busy. "Let me do my job, and quit worrying about me." She moved away from him and took orders for drinks.

The Brotherhood Protectors had employed her brother, Devin, when he'd come off active duty, medically retired due to an injury that had left him with a limp. He and his team had saved her life and that of her friend Mallory when an insane man, bent on revenge, captured them and buried them alive in fifty-five-gallon barrels.

After being tortured in Syria and then buried in a barrel, she should be afraid to leave her apartment, cowering in a closet or, at the very least, cocooned in bubble wrap.

However, Laurel didn't want to live her life looking over her shoulder, afraid to step outside and suspicious of every person who came within ten feet of her. She might as well have died in that hole in Syria.

But she hadn't. So, her waking memory was a little vague about what had happened to her during her captivity. She didn't even remember being carried out of the underground tunnels where her team had been held.

What she could remember from her nightmares was being naked and trapped in a dark hole, unable to move. So cold and alone. On the verge of giving up in her nightmares, she heard a deep, rich voice saying, "It's okay. I'm not going to hurt you. Let me help you out of there."

Strong arms lifted her out of the hole and gently wrapped her damaged body in a big shirt still warm from his body heat and smelling of...

She couldn't place the scent—woodsy...musky... pure heaven.

"Hey, Blondie," a voice called out.

The sound yanked her out of the tunnel and back into Gunny's Watering Hole, filled with hungry and thirsty cowboys, hopped up on adrenaline from riding bulls and broncos all day.

"Sir?" She pasted a smile on her face and looked at the heavy-set cowboy at the table beside her. "What can I get for you?"

"I was going to ask for one of Gunny's onion burgers, but a lap dance sounds even better," he said, pulling her down on his thick thighs and leering at her, his breath smelling of whiskey.

"Junior!" RJ came out from behind the bar, carrying a taser. "What did I tell you about touching the waitresses?"

"Oh, I was just playing." He patted Laurel's knee, his hand sliding up beneath her denim skirt.

In a split second, Laurel went from a calm, happy waitress to a fighting, kicking, hissing animal. She leaped from the man's lap and shoved him backward until his chair tipped over, sending him slamming down on the barroom floor. Then she leaped onto him and pounded his chest.

The man gripped her wrists to keep her from scratching his face.

Rational thought flew out the door as she fought for her freedom and her life.

"Laurel," a voice called out.

She could barely hear through the buzzing in her ears.

As the meaty hands holding her wrists tightened, she fought harder, finally jerking them free and scrambling to her feet. She turned in a circle, surrounded by men, all staring at her.

Her chest tightened, and she threw herself under a table and curled into a ball. She was back in the torture room, surrounded, naked, and so scared she couldn't move. She closed her eyes and wished she was invisible or that she could disappear.

"Laurel," a woman's voice spoke softly. "Open

your eyes, Laurel," she coaxed. "It's me, RJ. You're safe. Come on. Open your eyes."

"Laurel," a familiar voice called out. "Come out from under the table, and let me take you home."

She opened her eyes and stared into pretty green eyes. "RJ?"

"Yeah, sweetie. I'm here for you," she said.

"Me, too." Her brother was on his knees in front of her, as was RJ.

Laurel frowned. "Why are you two on the floor?" She looked up, and her frown deepened. "Why am I under a table?" Understanding dawned on her. "What happened? What did I do?"

RJ chuckled. "You gave someone what he deserved." She held up her taser. "I didn't even need to use this on him."

"Oh, RJ." Tears welled in Laurel's eyes. "I'm so sorry."

"No, really." RJ touched her arm. "He deserved getting knocked on his ass and pummeled for putting his hand up your skirt."

"I'm so sorry." Laurel crawled from beneath the table and stood, smoothing her hand over the denim skirt. "I might be more help in the kitchen."

"You should go home with Devin and get some rest," RJ said.

"See?" Devin said. "I'm not the only one who thinks you need to live with someone rather than staying in your apartment by yourself."

"I'm not changing my mind." Still, she didn't want to be alone yet. Not after the drama she'd just performed.

Laurel pushed past RJ and Devin and then through the crowd of onlookers, forcing her way through to the kitchen.

Grizzled old Gunny gave her a gentle smile. "Miss Laurel, was the crowd out there getting to you?" He flipped a burger and laid a slice of cheese over it.

"Sure," she said. "Do you need anything from the lodge?" She needed to walk and breathe fresh air, out in the open.

"I could use more napkins. We've run out in here. I have a case in the walk-in pantry in the lodge kitchen. If you're going, could you pick up four bags? That should hold us over for tonight, and I'll bring over more tomorrow."

Ready to explode if she didn't get away from people in the next two minutes, Laurel dove for the door, burst through and ran down the lighted pathway toward the lodge. Tears filled her eyes and streamed down her face.

She'd told Devin she was okay, happy, over the past.

But she wasn't.

Her reaction to Jr.'s touch had sent her over the edge into that dark place she couldn't climb out of.

Though tears blurred her vision, she didn't slow, running as hard and fast as she could. No amount of running, no amount of distance could get her away from the demons of her past.

So desperate to escape her nightmare, with eyes filled with tears, she couldn't see in front of her until she hit a wall.

Her chest connected first, and then her face, slamming into something hard. When she bounced back, steel arms wrapped around her, trapping her against the wall.

Rational thought fled, replaced by her fight-or-flight instinct.

Laurel struggled to free herself, kicking, bucking, twisting. With her arms pinned to her sides by iron bands, she couldn't punch or gouge eyes out.

Terror gripped her as tightly as the arms around her, squeezing the air from her lungs. She couldn't talk, scream or beg for mercy.

Suddenly, she went limp. Before her captor could react, Laurel slipped to the ground, tucked and rolled into the woods, then burrowed into the brush. Her breath caught and held as she hid behind leaves, counting the seconds the dark-clad legs remained on the path.

Then those legs bent. The man they belonged to searched the brush for her.

All she could see was the silhouette of his head and hunched body.

"There you are," he said, his voice deep, smooth

and...familiar. A hand reached for her. "I'm not going to hurt you. Let me help you out of there."

Her heart stopped, started, stopped and raced to catch up with the oxygen she needed to think. The buzzing sound intensified.

"I'm not going to hurt you," he said. "Please, take my hand."

She knew that voice. It was the same one she heard every night in her dreams.

The buzzing faded. Her heartbeat slowed.

Laurel laid her hand in his palm. He might be a serial killer, but she didn't care as long as he kept talking to her...with that voice.

CHAPTER 3

Rico was surprised when the woman reached out to take his hand. After she'd gone bat-shit crazy trying to escape him, he was sure she would sink deeper into the shadowy woods and get lost.

He felt horrible for having scared her.

She'd been terrified.

He'd held on because he was afraid that if he'd let go, she'd have collapsed, slammed into a tree trunk or gotten lost. He hadn't counted on her going completely limp and sliding through his arms to the ground.

"It's okay," he said softly. "I won't hurt you. I just want to make sure you're all right.

Applying the slightest bit of tension, he pulled her out from under the bush and let her get herself to her feet.

When she swayed, he cupped her elbow lightly to steady her. "Can you stand on your own?"

She wiped moisture from her cheeks before looking up at his face.

A gap in the tree branches added starlight to the soft glow of the lights lining the path, shining down into her face, glinting off eyes so blue they looked as if they were made of starlight themselves.

Rico stared down at her, a memory tugging at his heart.

The petite blonde wore a denim skirt with a white blouse tucked into the waistband. Her hair hung down to her shoulders, straight and thick, cut in a straight line all the way around. He didn't recognize her hair or face, but those eyes...

"Do I...know you?" he asked.

Her brow puckered as she stared up at him, canting her head to one side. "Are you from Fool's Gold?" She smoothed her hand over her skirt and brushed leaves from her white blouse.

He shook his head. "No. I'm new here. I just hired on with Jake Cogburn and—"

"—the Brotherhood Protectors," she finished.

He smiled. "Right. You work with them?"

The woman shook her head. "No. I run a florist shop in town. My brother, Devin Layne, works for them. He said there was a new guy at the lodge. I take it you're the new guy."

"Yes, ma'am."

"What branch of service?" she asked.

"Navy."

"SEAL?"

He nodded. "How did you guess?"

"They like to hire guys with training and experience in special operations."

Rico cocked an eyebrow. "Your brother?"

"10th Special Forces. Green Beret," she answered.

Rico held out his hand. "Enrico Cortez. A pleasure to meet you. Sorry if I hurt you."

She laid her hand in his for the second time and gave him a crooked smile. "My fault. I should've been looking where I was going. I'm Laurel."

"Laurel," he said, rolling her name over his tongue. It suited her. "I was headed for the bar. Would you care to join me?"

When she hesitated, he added, "You'd be doing me a favor. I don't know anyone but Jacob."

She grimaced. "Can't. I'm working. I was just going to the lodge to get some napkins for Gunny." Her eyes narrowed. "Have we met before? I don't recall seeing you in town."

"Ever been to San Diego?" he asked.

She shook her head. "Fort Sam Houston?"

He shook his head. "Is that where your brother was stationed?"

"No. *I* was stationed there."

"Prior military?" he asked.

"Army," she said and looked past him. "I really

37

need to get the napkins for Gunny." She stepped past him.

He fell in beside her. "Do you mind if I walk with you?"

Laurel set off. "Weren't you on the way to the Watering Hole?"

"I was," he said. "I don't mind taking a detour. I promise not to slow you down this time."

Her lips pursed. "I should've been looking where I was going."

"Hard to do when you're running full speed and your eyes are leaking," he said softly.

Her head dipped, her hair falling across her cheeks, hiding her expression from him. "I had something in my eyes."

"Right." He didn't push for more. She obviously didn't want to talk about what had upset her. It was enough to walk beside her to the lodge to make sure she was okay and didn't run into anyone else. "You were in the Army," he stated. "What was your MOS?"

"I was a nurse."

"And now you sell flowers?" He shot a glance at her. "I thought once a nurse, always a nurse."

She looked at him with one eyebrow cocked. "What about you? I thought once a SEAL, always a SEAL."

"It's true. Just because you leave the Navy doesn't mean you quit being a SEAL." He frowned. "Laurel." Again, he rolled her name on his tongue, trying to remember if he'd ever dated a Laurel. "Do you have the same last name as your brother?"

"I do," she answered. "Why do you ask?"

His gut clenched. He pressed a hand to his belly, his head spinning with the possibility, flashes of memory hitting him square in the chest. "No reason," he forced out.

When they arrived at the lodge, Laurel climbed the stairs to the wide front porch.

Rico followed out of morbid curiosity, his steps slowing, his heart in his throat, his hands suddenly clammy.

It couldn't be... She looked nothing like... But then she'd been dirty...head shorn... The world wasn't that small... Was it?

Memories rolled through his mind like a disjointed movie.

The Syrian village clinging to the side of a hill, bathed in the soft glow of moonlight. A spider hole. The tunnel. A cell with a naked, beaten man. Another prisoner with slashes across his back. A hole in the ground.

Blue eyes shining up at him.

Flames.

Bert's last words.

Halfway across the dining room, Rico stopped and leaned against a table, struggling to walk, to think, to breathe. His lungs were so tight he couldn't get air into or out of them.

39

Ahead of him, Laurel pushed through a swinging door.

Rico was glad when the door swung shut between them. He needed a moment or two to slow his racing heart, restore air to his lungs and remember how to function like a normal human being.

The door swung open seconds later, and Laurel leaned through, a frown denting her forehead. "Did I lose you?"

He shook his head and dragged a breath into his lungs. "I'm coming."

Her gaze lingered, her brow dipping lower. "You don't have to. I can take care of the napkins myself."

He straightened and cleared the knot in his throat with a strangled cough, then gave her a tight smile. "I've come this far. I can help carry the napkins."

Her frown lingered. "You look like I feel. Are you okay?"

"Never better," he lied and closed the distance between them.

Laurel held the door open for him to pass through and let it swing closed behind them. She hurried toward a door on the wall to her right and stepped into a spacious pantry.

Rico stood in the doorframe as Laurel reached for the top shelf where several bags of paper napkins were lined up in a neat row. Even standing on her toes, Laurel was four inches short of the bags. She tried jumping to snag one with her fingertips. When that didn't help, she placed her foot on the bottom shelf, gripped the edge of the shelf below the one with the napkins and pulled herself up. She grabbed for a bag of napkins, yanked toward her, lost her grip and fell backward.

Rico stepped forward just in time to catch Laurel in his arms.

"Oh!" She clutched the bag of napkins to her chest and blinked up at him. "Thank you."

"My pleasure," he said, holding her longer than necessary. When he realized what he was doing, he eased her feet to the ground.

Laurel weighed more than the filthy, pathetic creature he'd carried out of the compound that night over three years ago. That woman had been shaved, beaten, probably raped and starved.

Laurel was light to that other woman's darkness. Other than her bright blue eyes, she didn't resemble the ISIS victim who'd barely survived captivity.

"I can stand on my own," she said.

Immediately, he let go. Laurel grabbed his arm to steady herself, still holding onto the bag of napkins. "Okay, then. Next time, I'll remember to be prepared," she murmured.

"Sorry," he said, kicking himself for letting his memories drive his actions and make him forget where he was and how he should handle a woman— especially one who might have been traumatized so severely.

41

She stepped back, her gaze raking over him. "Are you sure you're okay?"

"I should be asking you that question," he said. "You were the one who ran into me on the trail and then hid in the shadows like a wounded cat." Which made sense if she was who he thought she was.

Her cheeks flushed a deep pink. "I thought you were attacking me."

He nodded. "I understand. I imagine it was hard to tell in the light when you're running, and there's something in your eyes." He reached over her head and plucked another bag of napkins from the top shelf. "Gunny must be pretty desperate for these napkins for you to run so fast to the lodge to get them." He handed the second bag to her. "How many do you need?"

"Four," she replied.

He snagged two more bags and turned to her. "I'll carry these." His gaze connected with hers.

She was looking at him with a wrinkle in her brow. "I feel like I know you."

He opened his mouth to tell her where he thought he'd encountered her, but the gut-wrenching nature of that event froze his lungs. It happened every time he dredged up the memories of that night. Rather than stand there with his mouth hanging open and nothing coming out, he shrugged and stepped out of the pantry. By then, he was able to drag in a breath. "We should get these to Gunny."

Rico marched through the kitchen, dining room and great room.

Her footsteps sounded behind him, hurrying to keep up.

A hand reached out to touch his arm, bringing his flight to a halt.

"We have met, haven't we?" she said. "Were you one of my patients? Was I rude to you? If so, I'm sorry."

He looked down at the hand on his sleeve as she balanced the bag of napkins under her arm.

His gaze met those blue eyes, and everything about that night so long ago hit him with the force of a runaway freight train. "Yes," he said through gritted teeth. "We've met. But you probably don't remember."

She shook her head, a frown. "Where? When?"

When he couldn't tell her, her fingers curled into his shirt sleeve. "Tell me."

His breathing became ragged, just like when he'd run through the streets of that village, carrying a thin, dirty creature, barely recognizable as human. "Syria. Three years ago. The night we pulled a nurse, a doctor and an anesthetist out of an ISIS compound."

Her eyes widened, and her face blanched. The bags of napkins dropped to the floor. "That was you?"

In his own living hell of memories, he almost

didn't move fast enough to catch her as her eyes rolled backward and her knees buckled.

Rico flung the bags of napkins he carried aside and lunged for her, catching her before she hit the ground. Swinging her up into his arms, he carried her back into the great room and lowered himself onto a leather sofa with Laurel clutched in his arms, draping her across his lap.

As she came to, he held her gently, forcing back the storm of emotions that inevitably overwhelmed him when he recalled that night.

Those blue eyes blinked open.

"It's okay," he said. "I'm not going to hurt you."

Tears trickled from the corners of her eyes. "It was you," she whispered.

Rico nodded. "I almost didn't recognize you from that woman I pulled from a hole in the ground." He brushed a thumb across her cheek, wiping away a stream of tears.

No sooner had he done that than more tears replaced them.

"Hey, you're okay." Her tears pulled at his heart. "You're not there. You're here in Colorado."

She nodded, and more tears slipped down her cheeks. "I thought I'd left the past behind," she whispered.

"And here I am to bring it all back." He brushed his lips across her forehead. "I'm sorry."

She pressed a finger to his lips. "Don't be. I can finally put a face to the voice in my dreams."

He liked the feel of her finger on his lips. "And I can put a face to the memory of incredibly blue eyes staring up at me from that hole."

She shook her head and swiped at the tears. "I asked for your name. They wouldn't tell me. It was top secret. All they could say was Navy SEALs were responsible for getting us out." She cupped his cheek. "Thank you."

He nodded, his chest tight. The loss he'd experienced that night was as fresh as when it had happened. So many times since, he'd relived the mission, second-guessing decisions made. No amount of retrospection would bring back his friend. Robert Ramirez was gone, his wife widowed and his children left without a father.

"I'd heard one of your guys didn't make it," she said softly. "I'm so sorry. It didn't seem right to sacrifice a life to save a life."

What could he say? It was worth it? It was their job to die for others? Those were the risks they took when they signed on to become SEALs?

In the end, Rico made no comment.

Laurel sat up.

He pressed a hand to her back to steady her.

"I'm okay." She turned and rested her feet on the floor. "Gunny needs those napkins."

"I can get them to him. You should stay here and rest."

She shook her head. "I need to keep moving. It helps."

"Not if you're running into people or passing out in a pantry."

She gave him a weak smile. "I don't usually do those things. I'm really a very stable person. It's just…" Laurel glanced away. "I thought I was better."

Rico's lips pressed into a tight line. "And then I showed up and threw you back in that hell hole?"

"It's not just you." She reached out and patted his leg. "Other things happened that set me back. Then I got word that one of the three people you rescued that night committed suicide."

Another punch hit Rico in the gut. "The doctor?"

Laurel shook her head. "No. Chris Monahan. The anesthetist. Thing is, I talked to him less than a month ago. He seemed fine." Her voice caught on a sob. "He'd suffered so much more than me or Dr. Estep." She met Rico's gaze. "I'm told they tortured him in front of the doctor and me to get us to talk. They wanted secrets. We didn't have any secrets to tell. They didn't believe us. Chris took the brunt of their torture." She glanced away. "At least, that's what they told me. I don't remember much of what happened."

"That's probably a blessing," Rico said.

"All three of us left the service. Chris, because he

was medically discharged. Dr. Estep and I left after our commitment was up. I couldn't go back, couldn't deploy. Not after…that."

Rico stared into the fireplace, where fresh wood was stacked, ready for a cozy fire to warm the guests. "I get it."

"It took a while to get over the trauma and adjust to civilian life." She gave him a crooked smile. "If it wasn't for Martha and the flower shop, I don't know what I would've done. I didn't want to go back to nursing. I'd seen too much. Lost too much."

Rico nodded to everything she said. "But you adjusted."

Laurel's lips twisted. "For the most part. Until recently." She pushed to her feet. "I just have to get through the next few days. Then I can get back into a routine of making people happy with flowers."

"What's happening over the next few days?" Rico stood. "Is it the rodeo?"

Laurel shook her head as she gathered the four bags of napkins. "In Chris's suicide note, he asked his wife to have his memorial here in Fool's Gold and for his ashes to be spread in the mountains." She met Rico's gaze. "Dr. Estep is coming in for the memorial, along with several more of the team that deployed together to Syria. It'll be a reunion of sorts."

Rico took two of the napkin bags from her. "Thus, the need to keep moving. If you're busy, you don't have time to think." He led the way to the door and held it open. "I'm at a loose end until Jake assigns a client to me. Can I buy you lunch or dinner? I'd like to make it up to you for slowing you down on the trail."

"I owe you for saving my life. You don't have to make anything up to me." Her brow furrowed as she passed through the door. "If you're inferring that I need someone to hold my hand through the next few days, forget it. I've come this far on my own. I'm not going to backslide into depression, and I'm not going to commit suicide. I'm happy, damn it."

Rico backed a step. "Whoa! I didn't mean to make you mad."

Laurel sighed. "My brother has been nagging me to move in with him and his fiancée. My friends show up all hours of the day and, sometimes, into the night. I don't need constant company or supervision."

Rico chuckled. "I'm not your brother, and we aren't friends—though I'd like to think we could be someday. I don't want to hold your hand—unless you want me to. I asked for purely selfish reasons. I'm new to the area. Jake's a busy man with a business to run and a dozen guys to manage. It's nice to have someone to talk to and show me around."

"I'm busy, too," Laurel said.

"Right. You're a florist. I'm sure you're very busy. Do you need someone to load and unload supplies or drive you around to deliver arrangements?"

She stared at him through narrowed eyes. "As a

matter of fact, my driver just left me for a job in Colorado Springs. With the rodeo in town and a convention going on at the casino, I've been swamped and doing my own deliveries. But you're new here. You wouldn't know how to get anywhere."

"No, but I could drive. You could hop out and deliver. And, like I said, I could also help load things. It might save you a little time, and helping you would give me a chance to get to know Fool's Gold." He raised an eyebrow. "You wouldn't have to pay me. I can't guarantee how long I'll be available, but a few days delivering flowers would help me and, hopefully, help you."

"Hmm." Laurel's frown deepened. She glanced down at the napkins and spun. "At this rate, Gunny's never going to get his napkins." She descended the porch steps and headed for the lighted path.

Rico followed. As they neared the Watering Hole, he said, "I guess that's a no."

She opened the back door, turned to face him, and said, "Four-thirty AM. Laurel's Florals on Main Street. Be there. I have a big shipment of flowers coming in at five and need help unloading."

He grinned. "I'll be there."

Laurel lifted her chin. "If at any time I suspect you're doing this out of pity—"

His grin broadened. "You can kick me out of the delivery van."

"Don't think I won't," she warned.

He snapped to attention and popped a sharp salute. "Aye-aye, boss."

She grabbed the two bags he carried and turned, shaking her head, her lips twitching on the corners.

Laurel entered through the back door of the Watering Hole and let the door slam shut before Rico could follow her into the kitchen.

He rounded the building, entered through the front door and found a seat at the far corner of the bar, hoping to catch glimpses of Laurel Layne as he drank a beer.

She didn't emerge from the kitchen the entire time he sat at the bar. He left after an hour and walked back to the lodge, aware of the time and the fact he had to get up at four in the morning.

He shook his head.

He'd come to Colorado to get away from the Navy, away from reminders that he'd failed to have Bert's back. How fucking ironic was it to run into the woman he'd pulled out of a hell hole in Syria at the expense of his friend's life? Was he insane to suggest helping her out at her flower shop? Did he want to stab himself in the heart every time he saw her? Pain was a reminder that he was alive and Bert was dead.

Though they were strangers, they had a lot in common.

They'd both been in the military, spent time in Syria and had been shot at. They'd both lost someone they cared about and were wading through life trying to come to terms with PTSD. They were two very different people, fucked up by war.

His footsteps faltered halfway back to the lodge.

Maybe this wasn't such a good idea.

Laurel probably needed someone who wasn't as screwed up as he was. Someone who had his shit together and didn't have nightmares every damn night.

He should call and tell her never mind. It was a bad idea. Rico pulled out his cell phone to do just that.

Except, he didn't have her number.

He had to go to the shop the next morning to deliver that message.

Damn.

CHAPTER 4

THAT NIGHT, Laurel's nightmare was more detailed than any before. So much so she felt the pain of every beating and smelled the stench of burning flesh as her captors pressed lit cigarettes into her skin.

When a light shone down into her hole, and that warm, deep voice said, "It's okay. I'm not going to hurt you," she could see his face.

He pulled her out of the hole and out of the dream. She woke in the middle of the night, drenched in sweat. Free of the hole. Free of her captors. Free of one of the shadows that had clouded her mind for the years since her liberation.

For once, she didn't dread going back to sleep. The image of Rico's face and the memory of his arms wrapped around her made her feel safe enough she could close her eyes again and not fall back into the hell of her dreams.

Laurel slept soundly until her alarm woke her at four in the morning. She rose, stumbled into the bathroom and splashed water on her face to help clear the sleep from her eyes. The few hours of deep sleep had felt so good, she hadn't wanted it to end.

A glance at the clock on the counter made her heart flutter. In fifteen short minutes, Rico would be at her door, ready to go to work with her. Her pulse quickened, and her breathing grew a little erratic as she brushed her teeth, pulled her hair up into a messy bun and applied a little mascara to her blond lashes.

She grimaced at her reflection. It wasn't much, but at least she didn't look like the wreck she'd been when Rico had rescued her in Syria.

Another glance at the clock made her squeak. Ten minutes until he arrived, if he didn't come early. Laurel yanked the T-shirt she slept in over her head and rushed to pull on her jeans. After a minute of digging through her dresser for a suitable T-shirt, she gave up and ran to the closet.

Not the blue chambray shirt. It was too faded and had holes in the sleeves. She shoved hangers aside until she reached the blouse Mallory had given her for her birthday. She hadn't worn it in the shop because she was afraid she'd ruin it by snagging or staining the beautiful powder-blue fabric with the tiny white and yellow daisies sprinkled all over it.

Lights flashed through the windows from the street below.

Holy hell. It was him.

She grabbed the pretty blouse, shoved her arms into the sleeves, buttoned the two buttons in the middle then dove for her shoes. After sliding her feet into the ballet flats, she threw open the door and ran down the stairs. As she neared the bottom, a figure appeared around the corner of the building, stepping into the light at the base of the steps.

Laurel was moving too fast to slow her momentum in time.

Instead of stepping out of her way, Rico caught her in his arms and swung her around to deflect the impact.

"Whoa," he said as he set her on her feet and released her. "You'll break your neck coming down the stairs that fast."

She pressed her palms to her heated cheeks, glad the light over the stairs wasn't so bright he'd see her blush. "Do you always step into the paths of running women?"

He chuckled. "Do you always operate at full tilt?"

Laurel grinned. "Rarely." She rubbed her hands down the sides of her jeans.

Rico nodded toward her chest. "Uh, you might want to finish dressing before you launch yourself down a flight of stairs."

A glance down at her blouse made her gasp and spin away. She'd been in such a hurry to get to the shop before Rico she'd forgotten she'd only buttoned two of the buttons on her blouse.

"I'm not usually this discombobulated," she murmured as she secured the remaining buttons and shoved the hem into the waistband of her jeans.

"Discombobulated?"

Fully dressed, Laurel turned to find Rico grinning. "You know...confused, befuddled, hairbrained."

"I know what it means," he said. "I've just never heard anyone actually say it aloud."

Laurel lifted her chin. "I like the word. It doesn't get nearly enough airtime, and it's just quirky enough to make me happy." She ducked past him and hurried toward the back door of the flower shop. "The truck will be here shortly. I could use some help clearing tables and floor space to receive the delivery."

"Lead the way," Rico said and followed her into the back of the flower shop.

Between them, they moved empty boxes and buckets to make room.

The delivery truck arrived at five. They moved the fresh flowers into the shop, organizing them by type and color, placing them in buckets and vases filled with water to keep them fresh for as long as possible.

After the truck left, Laurel carried bunches of flowers from the shop's back room up to the front and placed them in more decorative buckets and vases on tiered shelves, wiping away water stains and cleaning up fallen leaves.

By six-thirty, she had the flowers where she wanted them and started working through the day's orders of arrangements.

"I'll be busy for a few hours making the arrangements we'll need to deliver. You don't have to hang around."

He glanced around the shop. "What a difference fresh flowers make."

Laurel smiled. "I love them. All the colors, smells and choices make me happy."

His gaze met hers, his lips tipping upward on the corners. "I'm sure they make your customers happy as well."

"That's what I aim for." She brushed her hands together. "I'd better get started. My assistant arrives at nine. She'll run the shop while we're out delivering."

"What do you do for breakfast?" he asked.

Laurel shrugged. "Sometimes, I drink a soda. I'm usually too busy to bother."

He frowned. "We're going to bother today. Who makes the best breakfast in Fool's Gold?"

Laurel didn't have to think about her answer. "Mattie's Diner—and you're in luck. It's next door." She glanced at the clock on the wall. "It should be open by now. You'll love Mattie. She's a sweetheart. She sends over food when she's not swamped."

"Any preferences?" Rico asked.

"Two eggs scrambled, bacon instead of sausage, one pancake, extra syrup, hashbrowns, extra crispy and a cup of coffee. Black."

Rico laughed. "I love a woman who orders with absolute conviction."

Laurel covered her heated cheeks with her palms. "I've learned life can be short. I go for what I want."

"I might need to write that down." Rico glanced around the shop.

"No need," she said. "Just tell Mattie you want Laurel's usual."

"Roger." Rico walked toward the back door.

"Wait," Laurel called out.

He turned with a grin. "Did you want to add to your usual?"

Laurel's stomach turned flips at his casual smile. The man was far too attractive for her own good, considering Laurel wasn't in the market for a relationship. Ever.

"No," she said. "Never mind. You can go."

She'd really hoped she could get on with her life, find a man to love and who could love her, no matter how damaged she was.

She'd even started dating recently, only to discover the man she'd been dating wasn't interested in her for any other reason than to get revenge on her brother by killing her and her friend Mallory.

Laurel shuddered at that memory her mind

hadn't blocked. Trapped in a barrel and buried, she'd been seconds away from running out of air.

Finding someone interested in her had been too good to be true.

What man would want a woman like her? She managed to hide most of her scars beneath her clothes. What would he think when there were no clothes to hide behind?

Then there were the scars inside. Mental and physical. No man had touched her intimately since Syria. She wasn't sure how she would react if someone tried to make love to her.

Based on her response to Junior putting his hand up her skirt, she might not respond well.

Then there was her medical evaluation post-captivity, where the doctor had revealed what her memory had refused to divulge. She'd been raped so violently that infection and scarring would likely result in infertility. She'd never bear children.

Though she'd always dreamed of being pregnant, having babies and nursing them with her own breast milk, Laurel had resigned herself to that loss. She'd found comfort in the idea of adopting children who needed a loving home and family.

Despite all that was wrong with her life, Laurel chose to find the beauty in living, to choose to be happy, even if all her dreams didn't come true. That meant avoiding situations that would cause her heartache.

Like falling in love.

Rico, with his knee-melting voice, impossibly broad shoulders and brown-eyed gaze a girl could fall into, had heartache written all over him.

Why had she invited him to help her?

Having him spend the day with her, driving her around Fool's Gold, wasn't avoidance of a potentially heartbreaking situation.

As soon as he returned, she'd tell him she didn't need his assistance. He could go back to the lodge and help RJ and Gunny with their guests, there for the rodeo.

Laurel threw herself into her work. The beautiful arrangements she created usually made her happy.

Knowing she had to send Rico away stole the joy out of her work and left her anxious. Every little sound out of the ordinary made her jump and spin toward the back door.

She didn't open the shop to customers until nine o'clock, allowing her the time she needed to make arrangements for the orders due that day.

Carissa, her assistant, wasn't due for another hour.

When a knock sounded on the back door, Laurel jumped. Her heart raced as she hurried to open the door.

Rico stood on the other side, carrying two covered plastic plates with a paper bag stacked on top. "Mattie apologized for taking so long. She had a tour bus of senior ladies unload right before I walked into the diner." He grinned. "Some of those ladies were a hoot. I was propositioned twice, and one woman wanted to adopt me."

Laurel opened her mouth to tell him he needed to leave, but the thought of Rico surrounded by gray-haired, naughty grandmas tickled her funny bone and made her giggle, releasing the tension that had been building since he'd walked next door.

She stepped aside, allowing Rico to enter, knowing she was only delaying the inevitable. This man had rescued her. He was her hero, carrying her to freedom when she'd almost lost hope. Falling in love with him would be too damned easy.

Laurel cleared a spot on her worktable and dragged up another stool, placing it beside hers.

Rico laid the two plates in the space provided and opened the paper bag, pulling out two plastic bottles of orange juice, plastic forks and knives and packets of syrup and butter.

The scents of bacon and pancakes wafted through the room, making Laurel's stomach rumble. She hadn't realized how hungry she was until Rico had set the plates in front of her.

He removed the covers and handed her one of the forks and knives. "Bon appetite."

"Thank you," she said and dug into the scrambled eggs, filling her mouth to keep from having to come up with something to say. Usually, she could talk to anyone. Why she found it difficult to converse with Rico was a mystery.

Her inability to think could have had something to do with their proximity. Every time Rico moved on the stool, his knee brushed against Laurel's. She could barely choke down her food.

Rico ate a few bites of his stack of pancakes, chewed and swallowed. "I've been thinking about this memorial event for your friend."

Laurel swallowed hard, forcing down a chunk of pancake. "What about it?"

"Is it open to the public?" he asked.

"I imagine so. I can verify with Chris's wife when she arrives today. Why?"

He glanced across their plates at her. "I'd like to go."

"Why?" she repeated. "You didn't know him."

"I didn't know him, you're right. But I've known guys like him. We're all brothers." His lips twisted. "Or sisters." His brow puckered. "We served. That makes us family."

Laurel stared at him for a long moment. He was right. Whenever she met others who'd served in the military, she felt that bond. "I'll ask his wife if it's okay."

"Thanks." He ate a few more bites of his pancakes. "You said you're having some sort of a reunion? Where?"

Laurel shrugged. "I don't know that they've identified a place. Only where the memorial will be held. His wife arranged to have the service in the Divine Chapel in two days. Most people are coming in tonight or tomorrow, based on the messages I've seen come across the group texts."

"How many people are coming? Do you need to reserve a place for the gathering?"

"I hadn't really thought about it." At first, Laurel hadn't wanted to think about it. "I think between Chris's wife, Dr. Estep and maybe three others, there are only six of us. I don't think we need to reserve a meeting room."

Rico shook his bottle of orange juice. "What places would work?"

"There's the Bottom of the Barrel Tavern and the Lucky Strike Casino." Laurel stirred her fork in her scrambled eggs. "The tavern has a back room, and the casino has meeting rooms you can reserve."

Her eyes narrowed as she thought about how the gathering might go. God forbid they got emotional, especially in places where people wouldn't understand.

Laurel shook her head. "No. Not the casino or the tavern. The only logical place would be Gunny's Watering Hole. There's plenty of room, and it's owned and operated by a fellow veteran. Not to mention, the majority of the staff is made up of veterans." She gave Rico a crooked smile. "As you know, the Brotherhood Protectors fill in where needed." She pulled out her cell phone. "I can clear it with Gunny, then let the group know."

She sent a text to Gunny, who responded immediately with YES. Drawing in a deep breath, she sent a text to the group, letting them know to meet the following night at seven at Gunny's Watering Hole. Once she hit SEND, she released the breath she'd held and rubbed a hand across her chest in an effort to ease the tightness.

Rico reached out and took her hand in his. "It's okay. It'll be just another day."

Laurel squared her shoulders. "Speaking of just another day... Let's load the van and make the deliveries. I'd like to get back to the shop and help Carissa with tomorrow's orders and any walk-ins that might wander through."

With Rico's help, Laurel had the van loaded in ten minutes with all the flower arrangements that had been scheduled for that day's deliveries.

When Laurel's assistant pushed through the back door, she carried her usual steaming insulated mug of coffee.

Laurel waved a hand toward Rico and made hasty introductions. "Carissa, this is my temporary driver, Rico Cortez, Navy SEAL, just signed on with Jake Cogburn and the Brotherhood Protectors."

Before Carissa could say anything, Laurel waved toward Carissa. "Rico, this is Carissa Spangler, my assistant and right arm for the past year. Don't scare her off. I can't do this on my own."

"Aye, aye!" he said with a smile and shook Carissa's hand. "Nice to meet you."

"Oh, believe me," Carissa's gaze swept Rico from head to toe, "the pleasure's all mine."

Laurel's fists bunched at the obvious interest in her assistant's eyes. "The shop opens in five minutes. Can you handle it?"

Carissa's gaze darted to Laurel, her brow furrowing, making Laurel feel bad about her snarky tone. "Of course," Carissa said. "Enjoy the morning." The younger woman's gaze slid over Rico, and she smiled. "I know I would."

Laurel left the shop, shaking her head. She should have expected Carissa's reaction to Rico. The man was hot. Carissa was guy-crazy and never missed an opportunity to flirt.

Laurel didn't have time to flirt with her temporary driver. She had a business to run.

Or so she told herself.

Flirting was off the table. She didn't want to encourage any man when she had no intention of sleeping with him. And didn't most men date so they could sleep with the woman at some point?

Unless, like Alan Croft, they wanted to kill the woman.

Yeah. She was better off permanently single.

Using a GPS map application and Laurel's intimate knowledge of the place where she'd lived most of her life, they made the deliveries in record time.

Laurel also filled Rico in on some of the long-time residents, recent challenges and upcoming events.

The deliveries always brought her joy to see the happiness on the faces of the recipients. She smiled and chatted briefly, especially with the elderly.

Their final delivery was to the casino.

"We have a contract with the casino," Laurel said, then instructed him to pull around to the loading dock. She jumped out and went inside for a rolling cart. When she came out, Rico had the back of the van open and half the arrangements moved to the top of the ramp. They loaded all the items onto the cart.

"Wait just a second." Rico leaped off the dock, then closed and locked the van, pocketing the keys. He joined her on the dock. "I'm coming with you."

He pushed the heavily laden cart into the casino, following Laurel from point to point.

While Rico removed the old arrangement, Laurel replaced it with the new one.

When all the new arrangements were set in place, Laurel turned to Rico.

"What do we do with the old ones?" he asked.

"We take these back to the shop and reuse the containers on the next delivery unless the manager requests new vases or the vase is cracked."

"Smart reuse of supplies," Rico said as he wheeled the cart toward the rear of the casino.

"Many of my customers bring vases back to the shop, not wanting to keep a dozen empties in their cabinets. "I give them a discount on their next order." She laughed. "Kind of like pop bottle returns."

He shot a glance at her. "You have a beautiful smile."

She raised a hand to her heated cheek. "Thank you." *Too bad the rest of me isn't as beautiful*, she thought. Not that it mattered. This man would never see her naked.

As Rico pushed the cart down the ramp to the van, Laurel paused at the top, admiring the view.

The Navy SEAL had broad shoulders, narrow hips and a natural swagger that couldn't be faked. His thick, brown-black hair was short on the sides and longer on top, with a wave that made Laurel want to run her fingers through it.

When he glanced up at her and smiled, her heart fluttered, and her knees grew weak.

His smile turned upside down, and a frown pulled his eyebrows together in a V. "Are you okay?"

"I'm fine," she replied. In reality, she wasn't.

The last man she'd dated hadn't gotten past a good-night kiss.

No loss there.

He'd turned out to be a raving lunatic who'd tried to kill her and Mallory.

Not that Rico would do the same. Jake Cogburn hired only the best, most reliable men for the Brotherhood Protectors.

That wasn't the problem.

She was the problem. She had scars on her back and feet from the beatings. Her ISIS captors had used leather straps and skinny sticks, creating a crisscross pattern over her shoulders and back. If that wasn't bad enough, they'd burned her with lit cigarettes on her thighs and even her scalp after they'd shaved her head. When her hair had grown back, she'd been able to hide those scars.

The burn marks on her thighs, she hid beneath her clothes. But they were the ones that reminded her of the other ways they'd tortured her.

Yeah, getting naked with a man now was not something she was ready to do. But she wouldn't mind seeing Rico naked. She bet he wouldn't disappoint.

By the time she descended the ramp, he had all the old arrangements loaded in the back of the van. He closed the door and clapped his hands together. "Where to now, boss?"

"Grab lunch on the way back to the shop?"

Rico glanced at his watch and grinned. "Perfect timing." He held open the passenger door.

Laurel climbed in. "Perfect timing for what?"

"When I was at Mattie's, I placed a lunch order for one o'clock." He held out his wrist.

She glanced at his watch. It was five minutes until one o'clock. Just enough time to drive from the casino to Mattie's Diner.

"I wanted to get it to go and bring it back to the shop," he said.

He closed the door and rounded the back of the van to slide into the driver's seat. As he started the vehicle, he shot a smile in her direction. "I told her to make it to go."

Laurel frowned. "I always bring something back for Carissa."

Rico's grin broadened.

"Let me guess. You made it an order for three."

He nodded.

Laurel's frown lifted, a smile curling her lips. "You sure you want to work for Brotherhood Protectors? I could use a guy like you to keep me fed."

"Just trying to make a good impression with the boss on my first day." He winked, and the smile he turned her way melted like chocolate into every one of her pores. The heat winged its way to her core, making her squirm in her seat with naughty thoughts of licking melted chocolate off his naked skin.

Holy hell.

Laurel faced the road ahead, willing her body to calm the fuck down.

Rico was a temporary hire. Once Jake assigned him to a client, she wouldn't see much of him. Besides, she wasn't in the market for an...

Orgasm.

Laurel swallowed a gasp. Heat rising up her neck into her cheeks.

No.

Date. Relationship. Male friend. Buddy.

Not Orgasm.

Why the hell had that word popped into her mind?

Because, since he'd carried her across the floor in the lodge and sat her in his lap, she couldn't think of anything else.

As nice as his assistance had been that day, she should never have taken him up on his offer to help. She was quickly running toward a fire fueled by raging hormones.

Though she was a mess physically and mentally, her body and soul had all the normal needs and desires of any healthy, emotionally stable female her age.

She didn't need a man to satisfy herself sexually, she reminded herself. She could use sex toys that would achieve the same results.

Bullshit.

"Did you say what I think you said?" Rico glanced her way.

Heat filled cheeks. "Did I say something?"

"I could swear I heard you say bullshit." He chuckled. "Was there something I said or did that made you say that?"

"No, not at all," she rushed to answer. "I was thinking about something else."

"Anything I can help you with?" he asked.

Yes! That orgasm.

Laurel fought the devil on her shoulder and finally managed. "No. It's my problem. I'll deal with it."

"I'm pretty good at brainstorming solutions," he persisted. "Try me."

Oh, I'd like to try you, but...

"Oh, look," she said, pointing to the diner. "We're here. I'll run inside and get our lunches while you park the van behind the shop."

He'd barely pulled the van to a stop between the two buildings when she yanked open the door and jumped out.

"You sure you don't need help carrying the food?" he called out behind her.

"No. I don't need help," she said as she ran for the diner's front door.

Yes, she needed help. And yes, he could do wonderful things for her... But never in a million years.

She was too damaged to let anyone past the wall she'd built around her soul.

Rico Cortez deserved better than a broken-down victim of ISIS violence.

CHAPTER 5

AFTER LAUREL LEAPED out of the van, Rico sat for a few seconds until she disappeared around the corner of the diner.

"What did I say?" he asked aloud. "And what was she calling bullshit about?"

Women.

He drove to the back of the flower shop and parked the van near the back door.

As Rico stepped out of the van, Carissa opened the back door, holding a large trash bag almost as big as her.

"Let me get that." He hurried to take the bag from the petite redhead who couldn't be more than a teenager.

"Oh, thank you," Carissa said. "This is the first break I've gotten since you two left to do deliveries."

Rico took the bag to the big trash bin, tossed it in

and returned to help Carissa empty the van of the old arrangements.

They had the van emptied and another trash bag full of the wilted flowers when Laurel entered through the back door, carrying a stack of carryout-covered plates. "Anyone hungry?" she asked, a bright smile lighting up her face.

Rico still found it hard to believe this was the same woman as the creature he'd removed from a dark hole in Syria. How could someone who'd suffered as much as she had smile so brightly and make everyone around her happy just to be in her presence?

Carissa quickly cleared a worktable.

Rico carried the two chairs he could find to the table and held them as the two women sat.

Carissa frowned up at him. "What about a chair for you?"

Laurel frowned and started to rise. "Here, take mine."

Rico laid a hand on her shoulder. "Sit. I can stand."

Laurel's frown deepened as she glanced around the back of the shop. "There," she pointed. "Use that wooden crate. If you turn it on its side, it'll be just tall enough for you to sit with us."

He really didn't mind standing to eat, but he knew that if he didn't do as Laurel suggested, she'd get up and do it herself. It was in her nature to think more of the comfort of others than her own.

He moved a bucket of fresh flowers off the crate, flipped it on its side by the table and straddled it like a stool.

Laurel gave him that smile again. The one that made his heart skip beats and his groin tighten.

Rico would flip a hundred crates to keep her smiling. Too often, while they'd been driving around that morning, her smile had disappeared, and a frown had dented her brow. She'd appeared to be staring into the distance.

He'd wondered more than once if she was thinking about the past.

He recognized that faraway stare as one he got when a memory popped into his head and dragged him back into a battle or the extraction that had saved three lives and cost one.

"So, Rico..." Carissa opened her tray and wrapped her hands around half a club sandwich. "Are you staying at the lodge?"

He nodded. "I am. I want to see what the work entails before I start looking for a place of my own."

"So, you were a Navy SEAL," Carissa took a bite of her sandwich, chewed and swallowed. "I watched a documentary on SEAL training. I'm impressed to finally meet someone who made it through." She smiled and took another bite.

Feeling the need to say something, Rico asked, "Have you both lived in Fool's Gold all your lives?"

Carissa tipped her head toward Laurel. "Laurel has, except for her years in college and the Army. I didn't move here until my father got stationed at Fort Carson, down in Colorado Springs. He was an Army Ranger. He bought a house in Manitou Springs. I went to high school there, college in Boulder and landed a job teaching kindergarten here in Fool's Gold."

Rico looked from Carissa to Laurel. "Aren't schools in session now?"

Carissa laughed. "Yes, they are."

Laurel's lips twisted. "Carissa didn't much care for teaching a class full of—what did you call them?"

"Screaming meemies," Carissa said. "Don't get me wrong. I love kids. One or two at a time. But when you're outnumbered twenty to one..." She shook her head. "I did it for one school year. It was enough to convince me that I didn't want to do it again."

"Didn't you have to do student teaching to get your degree?" Rico asked.

Carissa nodded. "It was a clever trap. They lure you in by placing you with a teacher who has full control over the classroom. You think, *This is easy.* Next thing, you have a shiny new diploma and land a job with a classroom full of five-year-olds who have never heard the word *no.*"

Laurel laughed. "I can just picture you standing in the middle of them as they run around screaming."

Carissa nodded. "That happened on more than one occasion. I kid you not."

Rico chuckled. "It takes a special kind of person to teach little ones."

"Agreed," Carissa said. "And I'm not one of them. Thankfully, Laurel took pity on me and hired me as her assistant."

"She's been a huge asset," Laurel said. "As the town has grown, my business has grown to the point I can't do it all on my own. And I'm down a driver."

"I wish I could stay on as your driver, but…" Rico started.

"But you have a job that pays better than I can afford to pay. Plus, your skills would be wasted here."

"I don't know," Rico glanced around at the huge bunches of flowers. "I think I could be trained to make flower arrangements." He winked at Carissa. "It can't be harder than passing BUD/S."

Laurel laughed. "Hardly."

"Oh, I don't know." Carissa tipped her head toward Laurel. "You haven't trained under Drill Sergeant Laurel Layne."

Rico cocked an eyebrow. "Did your Army training come through on Carissa?"

Laurel's brow wrinkled. "Was I that hard?"

Carissa laughed. "Just kidding. I've never worked with a more positive, kind individual than Laurel.

She helped me get past the trauma and feelings of failure after that year in elementary hell. She's pretty amazing." She leaned over and hugged Laurel.

Laurel's cheeks filled with color. "You're pretty great, yourself. You just need to find your niche—one that makes you happy—and pour your heart and soul into it."

Carissa stared at Laurel. "I bet you were one hell of a nurse, and your patients all loved you." She shook her head. "I still can't believe you gave it up to arrange flowers for a living."

Laurel stiffened. "I found my niche," she said, her tone tight.

"Well, he must have been a real asshole for you to leave a profession that took some intensive training and coursework." Carissa took another bite of her sandwich. "It isn't easy to become a nurse. I wouldn't make it past chemistry. And then to go into the Army to use that training. You could've gone so many different places on the government's dime."

Rico met Laurel's gaze.

She gave an almost infinitesimal shake of her head.

Rico understood.

Laurel hadn't told Carissa about her captivity in Syria.

"To me, being a nurse in the Army was like you in that kindergarten class," Laurel said. "It was handling sick call for a bunch of privates who were nothing more than teenagers who'd been taught how to hold a gun."

Carissa grimaced. "The only thing worse than teaching a five-year-old is teaching a class full of high school kids who know it all."

Rico laughed because Carissa expected it. What he really wanted to do was pull Laurel into his arms and hold her. She'd made light of her exit from the Army. He'd bet that it hadn't been the sick-call soldiers that had driven her out. More than likely, it was the trauma she'd experienced at the hands of ISIS. Yet, she chose to smile and make others happy with the flowers she delivered.

Rico wanted to tell Carissa that there were a lot worse things than teaching five-year-olds in a heated and airconditioned building, knowing you could go home at night to people you know and love and not be beaten, raped, burned or thrown into a hole in the ground.

But he didn't say that.

Neither did Laurel.

She knew there were a lot worse things but kept it to herself.

She'd eaten a couple of bites from her sandwich and put it back on the plate.

A bell rang in the front of the shop.

"You two stay," Laurel said. "I'll get it."

She left the workroom and walked into the front

of the shop. "Welcome to Laurel's Florals. Can I help you?"

Rico wanted to follow, but after she'd ordered them to stay, he remained seated on the crate, his gaze on the open door between them.

"Laurel is the best boss," Carissa was saying. "She has the most upbeat personality of anyone I know. I don't know how she can keep smiling when people can be so cranky. But she does it. Every day. I want to be more like her."

The bell jangled again.

"Oh, sweet Jesus." Laurel's voice carried from the front of the shop to the back.

Rico sprang from his seat and strode to the door.

Several women stood beside a display of pale pink roses and carnations.

Just past them, near the door, a tall, thin man with salt-and-pepper gray hair held Laurel in his arms.

Her back was to Rico, so he couldn't see her face. Her shoulders shook as if she were sobbing.

Rico crossed the room in three long strides. "Let go of her," he said, his voice low and threatening.

The man's eyes widened. "Excuse me?"

Rico's fingers bunched into fists, and he raised his hands, "I said, let go of her," he repeated.

The man gripped Laurel's arms and set her away from him. "Do you know this man?"

Laurel turned toward Rico, wiping tears from her cheeks. "Oh, yes. This is Rico Cortez." She gave Rico a watery smile. "Rico, you might remember Dr. Richard Estep?" She glanced up at the doctor. "Richard, this is one of the Navy SEALs who rescued you."

Dr. Estep's face paled. "I'm sorry," he said. "I didn't recognize you." His eyes grew suspiciously glassy. He stepped toward Rico and engulfed him in a bone-crunching hug. "I never had the chance to thank your team for what you did that night."

Rico gently patted the man's back, remembering the thin, bare-chested man who'd refused to leave without Layne. He'd been the only one of the three who'd been strong enough to walk out on his own, despite having been starved and beaten. He'd had open slash wounds laced across his back and a bruised and battered face.

When the doctor stepped back to stand beside Laurel, Rico studied his face.

Estep didn't look much like the man they'd found in that cell three years ago.

"Were you the one who carried our nurse out?" the doctor asked.

Laurel answered for him, "He was. Could we not talk about this here?" Her gaze went to the women standing in front of the pink floral display. "Did you get my message about meeting at Gunny's Watering Hole?"

Dr. Estep nodded. "I'll be there. I heard from Bonaduce and Conley. They plan on coming tonight."

Laurel hugged the man around the middle again. "It's really good to see you." The skin between her eyebrows puckered. "Although the reason for coming together isn't great."

The doctor shook his head. "I wish we'd known he wasn't doing well. I hadn't spoken with him since Christmas."

Laurel shook her head. "I talked with him less than a month ago. He seemed fine. But then, a phone call isn't the same as going in person."

"Even then, you don't know what's going on beneath the surface." Dr. Estep sighed and glanced across at Rico. "I'm glad to get to meet one of the team who liberated us."

Rico dipped his head.

"I was sorry to hear about your guy who didn't make it out," the doctor continued. "Is it possible to get his home address? I'd like to send something to his family."

Rico's gut clenched. "I'd have to ask his wife. She took his death hard." He didn't go on to say that Ramirez's wife had just learned she was pregnant when the Casualty Notification Officer showed up at her door to deliver the news of her husband's death.

Rico had wanted to be there when the man came, but he'd been stuck at Landstuhl Regional Medical Center in Germany, fighting infection from the bullet that had nicked his calf on the way out of the village. He hadn't gotten back to San Diego in time to be there for Louisa and the kids when they'd received the news of Bert's death.

Louisa Ramirez had been so grief-stricken she'd miscarried her baby several days later.

Rico had arrived in time to take her to the hospital and stayed until she recovered enough to pack her belongings and move with her children to San Antonio, Texas, where her parents lived.

Rico had been so drained by the time Louisa left, his commanding officer had ordered him to bedrest and psychological evaluation and treatment.

During his ordered time off, he'd hidden out in his apartment for an entire day, jumping at every loud noise and pacing. The walls had seemed to close in around him. Finally, he'd left the building in shorts and his jogging shoes. He'd run until he couldn't run anymore. When he'd stopped running, he sat on a curb until a police car stopped, and the officer told him he couldn't loiter in that location, and that if he needed a place to stay, he knew of a shelter that would provide a hot meal and a clean bed.

The cop had thought he was homeless.

Rico had almost laughed. He couldn't blame the man for his assumption. He hadn't bathed or slept in days, his beard was scraggly and he smelled.

He'd thanked the officer and asked if he could use his cell phone. The man had let him have it and waited while Rico called TJ and asked him to pick him up.

He'd had to ask the cop where he was.

TJ had taken him back to his place, maintaining that Rico didn't need to be alone. Before he'd let Rico sit on any furniture, he'd herded him to the bathroom and told him not to come out until he'd taken a shower. "Jesus, you smell like toe fungus."

In a daze, Rico had showered and dressed in sweats TJ loaned him. Then he'd fallen into the bed in TJ's guest bedroom and slept for two days, rising only to relieve himself and eat whatever food TJ put in front of him.

When he'd woken on the third day, TJ handed him a cup of coffee and told him to get back to work.

For the next few years, he'd done his job, performed the missions, extracted good guys and killed bad guys. Through it all, he'd suffered nightmares of the night Bert had died.

"Have you heard from Chris's wife?" Dr. Estep asked Laurel, pulling Rico back from the Syria of his memories. Back into the flower shop with Laurel and the two ladies discussing the virtue of carnations over roses with Carissa.

Laurel shook her head. "I haven't heard from Chris's wife since she texted me a couple of days after Chris...died to tell me she was coming with his ashes and that she would appreciate it if I passed on the word about the memorial here in Fool's Gold in case any of his former Army buddies could come." She sighed. "That's when I called you. She'd given me all the information about the venue, time and date and that she would arrive today. I tried to contact her to see if she wanted me to come to California to be with her. She never returned my calls or texts."

"Did she give you her flight number?" Rico asked. "Someone could've driven to the airport to pick her up."

Laurel's lips pinched together. "She didn't return my messages. I can only imagine what she's going through."

The bell over the door jangled.

Everyone in the shop turned toward the woman who entered.

A tall, slender woman with auburn hair draped over one shoulder entered the shop. Her gaze skimmed over the people in the room, stopping when it reached Laurel and the doctor. Her eyes narrowed. "Laurel Layne?" she asked.

Laurel raised a hand. "That's me. Can I help you?"

The woman nodded. "Yes, indeed you can." She moved closer and held out her hand. "I'm Mandy Monahan, Chris's wife." She closed her eyes briefly. When she opened them, she did so without displaying any emotion. "*Was* Chris's wife.

Laurel took the woman's hand in hers. "Oh, Mandy, I'm so sorry about Chris. If there's anything I can do to help, all you have to do is ask."

"Thank you. I might need some help soon." The young widow gripped Laurel's hand for a moment.

Mandy took her time, holding on longer than necessary. After the first couple of seconds in Mandy's grip, Laurel's eyes narrowed, and her mouth tightened.

When Mandy released Laurel's hand, Laurel held her right hand in her left, slowly massaging her fingers.

Mandy turned to the doctor. "You must be Dr. Estep. I recognize you from the photos on Chris's old cell phone." She held out her hand to the doctor.

He took the hand and gave it an awkward shake. "I'm so sorry for your loss, Mrs. Monahan. We all loved Chris. He was the glue that held us together with his sense of humor and random factoids."

Mandy's eyelids fluttered. Her gaze shifted from the doctor to Laurel. "He would've been so happy for the both of you. You look great, like you're adjusting well to life outside the military."

Unlike her husband, who'd successfully committed suicide, leaving behind his widow.

Rico could almost imagine Mandy saying something like that.

Thankfully, they hadn't had any children.

"You'll both be at the memorial tomorrow?" she asked.

"Yes, ma'am," Laurel said.

Dr. Estep nodded. "Absolutely."

Mandy lifted her chin. "He spoke of you both and how he admired your capabilities and dedication. He was proud that you got on with life after separating from the Army. Unfortunately, he couldn't get past the nightmares and the physical damage he suffered. He could barely walk after what they did to his feet."

Laurel touched Mandy's arm. "I'm so sorry he had to go through all that. I still have nightmares."

"So do I," Dr Estep said. "You don't go through something like that without lasting effects."

Mandy snorted softly. "Some people can bounce back, like you and Laurel. Others just want the dreams to stop. Chris went to all the therapies the Army offered and some available in the civilian sector. None of them could banish the demons that plagued his sleep. He was so tired he did the only thing he could to rest once and for all."

Tears ran down Laurel's face as she hugged Mandy Monahan.

The widow stood rigid, unfazed and stoic as Laurel continued to hug her.

Rico figured Mandy might still be in a state of shock over her husband's death.

Laurel let go and scrubbed her hands over her cheeks. "I'm sorry. I had hoped to keep myself together." She laughed, the sound choking on another sob. "I'm failing miserably."

Rico moved closer to Laurel and slipped an arm around her, providing a measure of strength to hold her over until these people from her past left her shop.

Mandy smiled stiffly. "Well, I need to go check into my hotel. When they didn't have my room ready, I came here hoping to catch you. And it's a bonus running into you, Dr. Estep. I'll see you both tomorrow." She turned and left the shop.

Dr. Estep and Laurel's gazes followed the woman out of the flower shop.

Neither said anything, even after the door closed behind the widow.

Laurel leaned against Rico.

Carissa emerged from the workroom at the back of the shop and met with the two ladies who were looking at the different displays of flowers.

Dr. Estep took Laurel's hand. "It is really good to see you, Laurel."

She nodded. "Yes. It's good to see you, too, Dr. Estep. I need to get back to work, but I'll be at the Watering Hole tonight."

"Good. I'll see you there." He released her hand and left the shop.

For a long moment, Laurel remained in the curve of Rico's arm around her.

He liked the way she fit against his side and the way she smelled of flowers and sunshine.

If he wasn't careful, he could fall for this woman.

"Thank you for coming into Laurel's Florals," Carissa said as she escorted the two ladies to the door. "We'll deliver the flowers to your friend tomorrow. Come again soon."

Laurel smiled weakly at her assistant. "Thank you for handling the ladies."

Carissa nodded. "My pleasure." Her brow dipped. "Is everything okay?"

Laurel nodded. "Everything is as good as it can get. I'll deliver flowers tomorrow, but I won't be able to help tomorrow afternoon. I have to go to a celebration of life for a friend."

Carissa's brow dipped lower. "I'm so sorry for your loss. Don't worry about a thing. I can handle the shop on my own."

"I know you can," Laurel said. "I don't know what I'd do without you."

Carissa hugged her. "You're going to make me cry." She pushed away and squared her shoulders. "I'm going back to work. We still have a lot to do before we close."

"I'm coming," Laurel said.

Carissa disappeared into the back of the shop.

Laurel sighed. "This is going to be harder than I thought."

Rico tightened his hold around her waist. "You've got this. I'll be at the Watering Hole tonight if you need a shoulder to cry on or a wall to walk into."

Laurel laughed and shook her head. "Thank you. I might take you up on that."

"Hey, Laurel," Carissa stuck her head through the door. "A package came for you sometime today."

"What was in it?" Laurel asked.

"I don't know," the assistant said. "It had your name on it, not Laurel's Florals. I didn't open it."

Laurel crossed the room and took the package from Carissa.

Rico followed her, wanting to put his arm around her again, but held back.

Laurel stared at the package and then ran her gaze around the displays of flowers. "I love the colors and textures. They bring me such joy." As she looked around, she tore open the package and pulled out a black cloth. She looked down at it. "I don't remember ordering a black tablecloth."

"It's not a tablecloth," Rico reached for one end of the fabric.

Laurel held the other end. Between them, the cloth unfurled, the bottom edges falling toward the floor.

The solid black cloth had white designs across the middle with a white circle below with black lines and curls inside the circle.

Laurel gasped, her face blanched, and she dropped her end of the fabric.

Rico's gut clenched as he realized the black swath of fabric was a flag. The designs in white were Arabic letters.

This flag was usually associated with ISIS.

CHAPTER 6

LAUREL PRESSED her fingers to her mouth, her breath frozen in her chest. Her gaze shot around the shop, searching for whoever had delivered the package. She didn't see the beautiful flowers, just the shadows behind the shelves and buckets.

"Carissa!" she choked out. Swallowing hard, she started toward the back of the shop. "Carissa!"

Carissa appeared in the doorway holding a single pink rose, her brow pinched. "What's wrong?"

"Who delivered that package?" Laurel asked.

Carissa shrugged. "I don't know. I got busy with customers midmorning. It just showed up. I set it aside for you to open when you got back from the deliveries. Why? What was in it?" She looked past Laurel to Rico.

He folded the black fabric neatly and then met

Laurel's gaze. "I'd like to take this with me to the lodge."

Laurel's body trembled. "Yes. Please. I don't want it here."

"And the package." He bent to retrieve the package where it had fallen to the floor. "I'll be right back." He left through the front door.

"What was it?" Carissa asked, her face creased in worry.

"A flag." Laurel's gaze remained on the door through which Rico had disappeared.

"A flag?" Carissa shook her head. "I don't understand. The only people I know who fly black flags are pirates."

Laurel closed her eyes for a moment. Carissa was a good help in the shop, but she'd barely been outside the state of Colorado as an adult. "It's an Arabic flag associated with ISIS."

Carissa's brow wrinkled. "Why would someone send you an ISIS flag?"

"Good question," Laurel murmured as she wrapped her arms around her middle, willing the trembling to stop.

"Are you okay," Carissa asked, her voice soft. She wrapped her arms around Laurel. "You're shaking. I'm sorry. If I'd known that package would upset you, I wouldn't have given it to you. Please tell me you're all right."

The younger woman was distraught at upsetting her boss.

Laurel forced a confidence she didn't feel by squaring her shoulders and pushing Carissa to arm's length. "I'm okay. The flag was just a silly prank. We have work to do. Let's get to it." She forced a smile to her tight lips and marched into the workroom.

Moments later, Rico returned. He stood close to Laurel. "I put the flag in my truck."

"Thank you." Laurel handed a vase of pink and white roses to Carissa. "This needs to go in the refrigerator display out front."

Carissa took the arrangement into the other room.

Rico moved closer to Laurel. "I think we need to have the package checked for fingerprints," he said softly.

Laurel frowned and continued working with the flowers. "Why?"

"If the flag was meant as some kind of threat, we might be able to identify the culprit via the fingerprints and stop him before he goes further."

Laurel turned to Rico, tears welling in her eyes. "You think it's a threat?"

"Maybe."

"And what do you mean by *if he goes further*?"

Rico shrugged. "Maybe nothing. But I don't want to ignore the possibilities and be blindsided."

Laurel raised her hands. "Who would do this?"

"I don't know, but we need to figure it out."

"It's been almost three years, for God's sake." A single tear slid down her cheek. It pissed her off. Anger trumps fear, right? "Why now?"

She swiped the tear from her cheek and planted fists on her hips. "I've come too far to backslide into fear. If someone is trying to scare me, bring it. I'm not climbing back down in that hole. Or any hole, for that matter. Never again."

Another stupid tear rolled down her cheek.

"Damn right." Rico opened his arms.

Laurel knew it was a mistake to rely on this man. He wouldn't be around forever. And hadn't she vowed never to be helpless again?

Yet, she was drawn to him like a moth to a flame. She stepped into his arms and leaned her cheek against his chest. "I don't have time to play games with a lunatic."

"No, you don't." Rico stroked her hair gently, applying minimal pressure.

Laurel could escape his embrace easily. She didn't feel trapped. Leaning into this man was *her* choice. She found strength in that knowledge at the same time as she found strength in his arms.

"Laurel, there's a woman out here who wants to talk with you." Carissa passed through the door between the front and back of the shop. "Oops, sorry." Her assistant performed an about-face and marched back out of the workroom.

Laurel stepped back, her cheeks heating. "I'm coming." She scrubbed a hand over her face to wipe away any evidence of tears. Nothing could be done about red-rimmed eyes. Oh, well.

She shot a glance up at Rico, adding a weak smile. "Like I said. I don't have time to play games, but thanks for the shoulder to lean on."

Pasting a smile on her face, she entered the front of the store.

Mandy Monahan stood in front of the blue hydrangea blossoms, clutching a picture frame to her chest. She'd changed into sleek, dove-gray slacks and a silky white blouse since she'd been in the shop earlier.

"Mrs. Monahan." Laurel approached her. "What can I help you with?"

"I'm sorry to bother you again. I came in earlier with a specific task in mind and completely forgot about it." She sighed. "Since Chris's passing, I can't remember whether I'm coming or going."

"You're probably still in shock. Trauma has that effect on people." Laurel's first instinct was to pull the woman into her arms and hug her tightly. But something about the way Mandy Monahan carried herself stopped Laurel from following her instinct. She had the feeling Mandy wouldn't react well to having a stranger hug her. She erred on the side of giving the widow her space. "I was shocked when you contacted me about Chris's passing. I still can't believe he's gone."

"His suicide was a shock to us all," Mandy said. "I know it's short notice, but I'd like a nice arrangement of white lilies and roses for the table where I'll display his photograph." She held out the picture frame for Laurel to see. "It's a picture taken before he went to Syria. I'm sure he'd have wanted people to remember him as he was then, not the man who came back from hell."

The photo was of Chris, wearing shorts and a polo shirt, standing at a point overlooking a sparkling blue bay. He was looking over his shoulder with a grin at the person snapping the camera, happiness shining from his bright blue eyes.

Laurel smiled down at the photo, a lump forming in her throat. "That's the Chris I remember. He always had a smile, a joke and a kind word for everyone."

"Yes, he did," Mandy said. "Before he left for the mission to Syria. When he returned, he was a different man from the one I married."

Laurel nodded. "None of us were the same after all we went through." Her voice trailed off. After Sukkar had died during the operation they'd been forced to perform, the ISIS terrorists had blamed them for killing their leader. Laurel should've been thankful they hadn't executed them on the spot. Then again, she would've preferred a quick death to the days of painful cruelty. All three of them had been tortured. Chris had gotten the worst of it.

Laurel pushed the horrific images of the dark tunnels, festering wounds and flayed skin from her mind and focused on the widow in front of her. "Lilies and Roses?"

Mandy nodded. "Please. Nothing too big. It's not like we're draping a casket. I'll have his urn beside the photograph."

Laurel grabbed a pen and an order form, noting Mandy's request. "What time should we deliver?"

"The service is at three o'clock," she said.

"By noon, then?" Laurel offered.

Mandy nodded. "That would be soon enough."

"I'll coordinate with the church," Laurel said. "Is there anything else you need?"

"Chris said you talked a lot about Fool's Gold, Colorado, when you were at the mobile hospital. The way you described it made everyone long to visit. Especially him. When ISIS held you all, he dreamed about visiting your hometown. It gave him a reason to keep living."

Laurel fought the tears welling in her eyes. "Home seemed so far away." And it was. She'd given up hope of ever seeing Fool's Gold again.

Mandy nodded, "That's what he said. He'd just about given up hope. Then the Navy SEALs arrived and whisked the three of you out of harm's way." She snorted softly. "He was supposed to live happily ever after, safe at home with his wife and the baby I was expecting."

Laurel touched the widow's arms. "I was so sad to hear about the baby. You and Chris had gone through so much already. That had to be devastating."

Mandy lifted her head and stared out the front window of the shop. "That was three years ago. Sadly, the tortures Chris was subjected to rendered him infertile. We would never have babies of our own."

"Did you look into adoption?" Laurel asked and immediately shook her head. "You don't have to answer. It's not my business."

"Chris was on too many pain medications and treatments for anxiety and depression. No one would allow us to bring a baby into such an unstable environment."

"I'm so sorry," Laurel said.

"I guess all the doors that closed, the losses and changes, were too much for Chris. For the last few weeks before he...passed, he said he wished he'd gone to Fool's Gold to see the Rocky Mountains. He wanted his ashes spread somewhere near there."

"If you want to spread ashes in a national park, you have to get permission from the national park authorities. If you spread ashes on private land, you need the property owner's permission." Laurel smiled. "I happen to know the owner of the Lost Valley Ranch, just outside of Fool's Gold. He's a prior-service Marine. He'd give you permission to spread your husband's ashes there."

"That would be lovely." She gave Laurel a sad smile. "He was so thankful that you and Dr. Estep made it out alive." She waved a hand around the room full of beautiful flowers. "And both of you went on to live successful lives. It made him happy to know you were able to put the past behind you."

"I wish I'd known how sad he was," Laurel said. "I would've come to visit. If only I'd known."

Mandy shook her head as she stared down at her hands. "He was almost like his old self the day before, laughing, teasing and loving. I thought he was finally on the mend. I was going to get my Chris back."

She bit her bottom lip and lifted her head, her eyes filled with tears. "The next day, I had an appointment to get my hair done. When I came home, I found him lying in the bathtub with the curtain drawn. He shot himself but didn't want me to have to clean up a big mess." Her words caught on a sob.

Laurel pulled the woman into her arms. "I'm so sorry," she murmured, holding the woman in her arms. She wished she could fix this but could do nothing to bring Chris back. So, she held the sobbing woman.

When Mandy finally stopped crying, she straightened and wiped the tears from her cheeks. "I'm sorry. You'd think I'd be all out of tears. I've cried more in the last few days than I have my entire life."

"You're allowed," Laurel said. She wanted to cry along with Mandy but didn't think it would help the woman if they both fell apart.

Laurel's gaze searched the room for Rico and found him leaning in the doorframe between the front and back of the shop.

He pointed to her and gave the OK sign.

Laurel gave him an almost imperceptible nod. Yes, she was okay. Better than she'd expected. Knowing she had to hold it together in front of Chris's widow helped fortify her and made her hold strong.

Mandy stepped away, reached into her purse for a tissue and pressed it to her eyes and then her nose. "I need to go," she said.

"I'll deliver the flowers to the church by noon," Laurel assured Mandy. "We're having a reunion of the members of Chris's unit at Gunny's Watering Hole this evening if you feel up to joining us."

Mandy shook her head. "That was Chris's world. I wouldn't know anyone there, although I'm sure they'd all be nice." She raised her hand palm up. "And this is where I go when people are nice to me. I dissolve into tears." She shook her head. "No. But thank you." Her parting smile was watery at best. "Chris would've loved to have been there to see his old unit back together. He loved his life in the Army —" Her voice caught on a sob.

"—before Syria," Laurel finished. "I loved my life in the Army before Syria." She shook her head. "But not after. I couldn't do it anymore. I didn't even want to be a nurse anymore."

Mandy waved a hand at the flowers. "You landed on your feet. And you seem happy and successful."

"It hasn't been easy," Laurel admitted.

Mandy's lips pressed together. "But you did it. Congratulations. I'll see you tomorrow at the memorial?"

Laurel nodded. "I'll be there. If you need anything, you have my phone number. Call me."

"Thank you." The widow walked out of the shop, climbed into a silver sedan and drove away.

After Mandy left, all Laurel wanted to do was climb the stairs to her apartment and sleep for the rest of the day. She felt as though she'd been in a giant washing machine on a spin cycle. Every bit of her energy had been sucked out of her, leaving her limp and barely able to stand.

Rico crossed the floor and slipped an arm around her waist. "Come take a seat in the back." He led her to the workroom, where Carissa was busy laying out the flowers for an order.

"Oh, there you are." Carissa's brow furrowed. "You look like a ghost." She pushed a chair over to her. "Sit."

Laurel didn't argue. She sank into the chair and stared at the assembly table. "I need to work."

"Let me get you some water," Carissa said. She ran to the refrigerator on the back wall of the workroom and pulled out a bottle of water. When she handed it to Laurel, she said. "Just sit there for a few minutes until you feel a little more like yourself. You can tell me what needs to be done, and I'll do it."

"I do that anyway," Laurel said.

"Yeah, but you're usually doing stuff at the same time. This time, you get to watch and critique." She winked at Laurel. "Rico can help."

Laurel's brows rose. "Have you ever worked with flowers?" she asked him.

He grinned. "I have. Counting today, I've worked with flowers almost one whole day." He looked around the room. "At the very least, I can fetch and carry." He clapped his hands together. "You're the boss. Tell us what to do."

Laurel laughed at the eager expressions on Carissa and Rico's faces. "Okay, then. But only until I get my second wind."

She spent the next thirty minutes going over the orders they needed to prepare for the next day and what she'd need for the arrangement for the memorial.

Between Rico fetching and Carissa arranging, they made it through several arrangements and laid out everything Laurel would need for the memorial display.

By then, Laurel had consumed the bottle of water

and was feeling more like her usual self. She pushed to her feet.

When Carissa and Rico started forward, she held up her hand. "I'm fine. I've found that the best way for me to handle adversity is to keep busy, work and fill my life and the lives of others with beautiful things. Besides, I want to make the arrangement for Chris's memorial. It's my tribute for a man who died too young." She glanced at the clock on the wall. "Isn't it time for you to go home, Carissa?"

Carissa crossed her arms over her chest. "Trying to get rid of me?"

"No," Laurel said, then grinned. "Okay. Yes. You've done everything else. I only have this arrangement to complete before I call it a day."

Carissa's eyebrows dipped into a V. "Are you sure you're okay?"

"I'm fine," Laurel propped her fists on her hips. "Have you ever known me to fall completely apart?"

"No," Carissa said. "But you came close today. It scared me. You're always the rock. I've cried on your shoulders more times than I can count, and I've never seen you cry. Until today."

Heat filled Laurel's cheeks. "I'm sorry. I'm a little emotional over my friend's passing."

Carissa's lips pressed into a tight line. "Well, it freaks me out that some asshole sent you a black flag. I think you should come to sleep at my apartment tonight."

Laurel shook her head. "Thanks for the offer, but I'm not staying the night at your place. Besides, I have a reunion to attend tonight, and you probably have a date."

Carissa clapped her palm to her forehead. "Date. Oh my God, I forgot I have a date." She stared at Laurel through narrowed eyes. "Are you sure you're going to be all right? I can cancel my date. It's just Dustin. I've canceled on him before."

Laurel chuckled. "Won't he get tired of being stood up?"

Carissa shrugged. "He'll get over it. If he doesn't, that's okay. He's not the one."

Laurel tipped her head. "How do you know he's not the one?"

"You know..." Carissa drew in a deep breath and let it out. "When we kiss, I don't get all tingly inside. I mean, he's a good kisser, but there's no spark."

"Have you felt that spark with anyone else?" Laurel asked.

Carissa shook her head. "No."

Laurel shook her head. "Then how do you know it exists?"

"My mom said that when she first kissed my dad, she felt all tingly inside," Carissa's face grew soft, and a smile spread across her lips. "She knew in that moment that he was the one for her. I'm waiting for that tingly feeling."

"Then why date Dustin?"

"It's nice to have someone to go to dinner with." Carissa reached beneath the counter and pulled out her purse. "I don't like to eat alone every night. Since you don't want me here, I guess I'll go to dinner with Dustin. I'll see you in the morning." She turned to Rico, her eyes narrowing as her gaze swept over him. "Hmm. You wouldn't happen to want to kiss me, would you? I get all tingly just looking at you."

Rico held up his hands. "You're a lovely young woman, emphasis on young, but no, thank you."

Carissa sighed. "Didn't hurt to ask."

"Sweetie, you can't go around kissing every random guy you run into," Laurel said.

Her assistant cocked an eyebrow. "Why not? If he's willing and I'm willing, what does it hurt?"

Laurel shook her head. "There are some crazy people out there. Some guys might think a kiss brands you as his. I don't want to see you hurt."

Carissa gave Laurel a crooked grin. "Don't worry. I'm all talk. The right guy will come along someday. I just have to be patient and open to the possibilities. You should adopt the same philosophy."

Laurel snorted. "About kissing every man?"

"No, about being open to the possibilities," Carissa met her gaze and held it. "How many dates have you been on since you've been back to Fool's Gold?"

Laurel's mouth pressed into a thin line.

"Besides with that psycho Alan Croft?"

"None," Laurel admitted, fully aware of Rico in the room with them. How pathetic did she sound? Not that she expected Rico to ask her out on a date.

"Exactly." Carissa shook her head. "And the one time you actually did go out, you picked a guy who wanted to kill you."

"I was open to possibilities then," Laurel argued.

"You were desperate," Carissa said, her tone flat. "He took advantage of that. If you'd been dating sooner, you might not have played right into his hands. You need to shake it up."

"What I need is to have a background check done on any man I consider dating," Laurel murmured.

Rico grinned. "I have a top-secret clearance. Does that count?"

Carissa waved a hand toward Rico. "There you go. Be open to the possibilities. I believe this man just asked you out on a date. Are you going to blow him off or take him up on it?"

Put on the spot, Laurel sputtered, "I...I..." Then, she mentally kicked herself to get a grip. "Just because he admits he has a top-secret clearance doesn't mean he wants to take me out on a date." Her cheeks were on fire with embarrassment. "Go on, Carissa. You're jabbering, and I need to get this arrangement done and get ready for the reunion."

Carissa's eyebrows rose. She glanced from Laurel to Rico and back. "Hmm. Have you considered kissing Rico?"

Rico laughed out loud.

"Carissa!" Laurel threw a Styrofoam ball at her assistant. "Leave before I fire you."

Carissa caught the ball. "Just saying. Rico could be the one. All you have to do is kiss him once, and you'll know."

"I don't kiss the help." Laurel half-turned her back on Carissa and Rico. "And I don't believe you know 'the one' based on a single kiss. You need to take time to get to know someone to make sure you're compatible."

"Your parents are still together. When did they know?" Carissa demanded.

"I don't know," Laurel said. "I do know that they dated longer than for one kiss before they tied the knot."

Out of the corner of her eye, Laurel watched as Carissa turned to the only man in the room. "Rico, what about your folks?"

Most men would have run from the room with all the talk of love at first kiss.

Laurel was surprised Rico remained.

Not only had he remained, but he also had a big smile on his face. "My dad knew my mother was the one before the first kiss. He swears that when he first saw her across the room at a friend's party, he told his friend that he was going to marry her."

"Ha!" Carissa said. "See? Love at first sight exists."

"Go," Laurel said, her face on fire with all the talk

ELLE JAMES

of love and kissing. Her face wasn't the only part of her body on fire. "Please. I need to finish this, and you need to get ready for your un-date."

Carissa slung her purse over her shoulder and flounced toward the door as only a twenty-two-year-old could and not look silly. She opened the back door and looked back at Rico. "Let me know how it goes when you kiss her. I'm betting she gets all tingly."

Laurel wished the floor would open up and swallow her. She'd never been more embarrassed in her life.

After Carissa left, Laurel fussed with the arrangement, her hands fumbling, the hairs on the back of her neck standing at attention. Every fiber of her being sizzled with awareness of the man leaning against the wall. Out of the corner of her eye, she could tell he was watching her.

After snapping a third flower stem, she braced her hands on the table and drew a deep breath. "Your driving duties are over for the day. I won't need your help until tomorrow morning."

"I figured that," he said.

"You can leave," she suggested.

"I know."

Did she have to spell it out for him?

She turned, braced her hands on her hips and gave him a pointed stare.

The man was smiling. He knew he was having an

effect on her. Based on the way his lips twitched, he thought it was funny.

Her jaw set in a hard line. "I can't work with you looking over my shoulder. Please leave."

Rico's smile slid off his face. "I'm sorry if my presence makes you uncomfortable." He stepped closer and laid his palm against her cheek. "I'm worried about you."

Laurel closed her eyes so she wouldn't have to look into the rich brown depths of his gaze. She fought the urge to turn her cheek into his palm. "It's not your responsibility to worry about me. You're the driver, not my keeper."

"I can't help but feel responsible for your safety. I didn't pull you out of that hell hole in Syria only to have you terrorized here in the States." He brushed his thumb across her lips.

The spark of electricity that shot through her made her eyes pop open. She stepped backward so fast she bumped into a bucket of red carnations and nearly fell in.

Rico's hand shot out and grabbed her arm. He yanked her away from the bucket. She fell against his chest so hard it knocked the wind from her lungs. At least, that's the lie she told herself. All the air left her lungs as her soft breasts mashed against the solid wall of his muscular chest.

His arms circled her, holding her gently until she steadied.

Her fingers curled into the fabric of his shirt as she inhaled the intoxicating scent of Rico, a mix of a woodsy aftershave and the outdoors.

The electric shock of his thumb on her lips made her wonder if his lips would have that same effect.

As soon as that thought occupied her brain, she pushed back, stepping out of his arms. She wiped her hands down the sides of her jeans and stared at a vase of roses and carnations Carissa had arranged for the next day's deliveries. "You need to leave so I can get my work done."

"I will," he said.

Not expecting him to agree so quickly, Laurel's gaze met his.

"But if you need me, I'll be out back in my truck."

"That won't be necessary," she insisted. "I've lived in the apartment upstairs for the past three years. I can manage to get home by myself."

"That might be true, but this is the first time someone has sent you an Arabic flag. One associated with ISIS. It's a message. Until we figure out what that message is and who sent it, I don't think you're safe."

She shook her head. "I've taken self-defense training. I know how to get myself out of a tight situation."

"Did I hear that you were taken captive not long ago? How did your self-defense training help you then?" he challenged.

"That's different. We were drugged."

He nodded. "You need someone watching your back."

"No. I. Don't." She touched a finger to his chest. "Out."

He held up his hands. "I'm going. If you need me, I'll be in the truck, parked outside the back door."

She drew in a deep breath and huffed. "Fine. I might be here a long time."

"Then I'll be out there a long time." He backed toward the door. As he reached it, he stopped. "But first, I want to make sure the front door is locked."

"I can do that," she said.

"Okay. Do it." He stood his ground, his arms crossing over his chest.

"You're not going to leave until I do, are you?"

"No, ma'am."

Laurel spun and marched through the workroom into the front of the shop, twisted the locks on the door, flipped the sign in the window to CLOSED and marched back. "Satisfied?"

"A little. You know where I'll be." He stepped through the back door.

Laurel slammed the door behind him with a little more force than necessary.

"Lock the door," Rico's muffled voice called out.

"Kiss my ass," she said softly, twisting the lock as she did.

"I heard that," he said. "And the lock click. I'll just

be waiting out here as it gets dark. By the way, I'm not afraid of the dark. Much. Don't worry about me."

"I won't," she said, a smile curling her lips. Damn him for being so…

Frustrating?

Bossy?

Protective…and cute.

She really needed to fire him.

Before she did something stupid.

Like falling for him?

Yeah, that could never happen.

Not in a million years.

CHAPTER 7

RICO LEFT the flower shop and Laurel, only going as far as his truck. He climbed in and lowered the windows. It was past time for him to check in with Jake. He pulled out his cell phone and called the head of the Brotherhood Protectors Colorado division.

Jake Cogburn answered on the first ring. "How was your first day delivering flowers?"

"Interesting," Rico answered. "We might have a situation brewing."

"Yeah?" Jake said. "Tell me."

Over the next few minutes, Rico gave him a brief situation report, ending with, "Do you know where we can get fingerprints run on the package Laurel received?"

"You could turn it over to the sheriff's office," Jake suggested.

"It's not a crime to leave a flag in a package," Rico

pointed out. "We don't know if this is a threat or a prank."

"Sheriff Faulkner's a good guy. Former Special Forces. He'd take it seriously," Jake said. "We've worked together on some of our cases. Let me give him a call."

"I'd appreciate that. I have the package in my truck, along with the flag."

"Where are you now?" Jake asked.

"I'm sitting outside the back door of the flower shop." Rico grinned. "Laurel booted me out."

Jake chuckled. "She's stubbornly independent. Until we get a bead on the person who left the flag, you need to be her shadow."

"I'd already planned on it," Rico said. "Though she might not take kindly to me following her around."

"I'll talk with her brother, Devin," Jake assured him. "He might have some sway with her."

Rico's hand tightened on his cell phone. "Either way, she's stuck with me until we get this settled. Whoever sent that flag had to have known the effect it would have on her. When we find him—"

"We'll deal with him then," Jake finished. "First, we have to find him. I'll call the sheriff and let you know what he wants to do with the package."

"Thanks," Rico said.

"For the record," Jake said, "welcome to the Brotherhood Protectors. You've just received your first assignment. Your job is to protect Laurel Layne."

"Roger," Rico said. "Out here." He ended the call and sat for a moment, conflicted. On the one hand, his chest swelled at the trust Jake had in him to do the job.

At the same time, his gut clenched. Laurel Layne's life was once again in his hands. He'd rescued and protected her before in a lot more volatile environment. How dangerous could it get in the States?

Considering a psychopath had already attacked Laurel since her return home, the answer to that question was things could be pretty damned dangerous, even in the States. In Syria, they'd known who the enemy was.

Here in Fool's Gold, Colorado, they didn't.

One sneaky bastard bent on hurting Laurel scared Rico more than a battalion of ISIS.

Like it or not, he was now Laurel's shadow.

Thirty minutes passed with no sign of Laurel.

Rico wished he could see into the building to gauge how much more time it would take for her to finish the floral arrangement for Chris Monahan's memorial.

Just when he was convinced it was time to check on her, she stepped out the back door, locked it and turned to stare at his truck.

"Go home, Rico," she called.

"Sorry," he responded. "Can't hear you over the music." He turned up his radio.

Laurel rolled her eyes and climbed the stairs to her apartment, pausing to unlock the door.

Rico reached for his pistol in the console, then dropped down from his truck and took the steps two at a time to the upper landing. He reached the top as Laurel's hand twisted the knob.

"I can open my own door," she said.

He placed his hand over hers on the knob. "I know. But let me clear your apartment before you go inside."

She pulled her hand out from under his. "It's a tiny apartment. Isn't this a little bit of overkill?"

"Better to overkill safety than to get killed," he said. "Humor me, will ya?"

She rolled her eyes. "Fine. Check for the bogeyman."

"Thank you." He motioned for her to stand to the side of the door, out of range, should someone be on the other side, ready to blow a hole through the first person who stepped inside. "Stay back."

With the barrel of his handgun, he pushed the door open.

Laurel reached around the doorframe and flipped the switch, flooding the apartment with light.

Rico frowned. "I told you to stay back."

"You can see better if the lights are on," she said.

"And so can the bogeyman." He gave her a stern glare. "Stay."

"I'm not a dog," she murmured.

"A dog would follow instructions," Rico countered as he slipped into the apartment, his weapon held in front of him, his gaze darting around the studio apartment consisting of a living room, kitchen and bedroom all in one room with an open door leading into what appeared to be a bathroom.

Rico made quick work of checking the main room, looking under the bed and in a small closet. Then he ducked into the bathroom, pulling the shower curtain aside to check inside the bathtub.

"Did you find the bogeyman?" Laurel asked from the doorway to the bathroom.

He glared. "I thought I told you to stay."

"I was never really good at taking orders in the Army. Another reason I left the military. Can I get a shower now? Or do you still need to check the drain in case someone is hiding there?"

"Funny," he said. "For the record, all clear."

"You can go home now," she said. "I'm in my apartment. No one else is here."

"And you're due at the Watering Hole at seven o'clock for a reunion with members of your unit." He strode for the door. "I'll be in my truck to take you there."

Her brow dipped low. "You're serious?"

"As a heart attack." He glanced at his watch. "Better hurry or you'll be late."

Laurel lifted her chin. "I'm taking my own car."

He strode through the door, pausing to look back.

"Then I'll be waiting to follow you there." Before she could respond, he closed the door.

Something thumped against the door.

Rico suspected it was one of the pillows from the couch. He chuckled.

"Not funny!" Laurel's muffled cry sounded through the door.

He descended the stairs and paced the length of the building several times, pausing occasionally to do squats and pushups. Might as well get a workout in while he waited.

Lights shone between Laurel's Florals building and Mattie's Diner. A sheriff's department vehicle eased around the corner and pulled to a stop beside Rico's truck.

Rico rounded the vehicle to the driver's side as a man with salt-and-pepper gray hair eased out of the vehicle and straightened. "Mr. Cortez?"

Rico nodded.

The man held out his hand. "I'm Sheriff Jim Faulkner. Jake Cogburn said you had a package you wanted us to look at."

Rico took the man's hand. "Call me Rico. Mr. Cortez was my father." He grinned.

"Rico," the sheriff said. He leaned into his SUV and pulled out a pair of surgical gloves and a paper bag. "Show me."

Rico led the sheriff around to the passenger seat, where he'd deposited the packaging and the flag.

"Our fingerprints will be all over it, but maybe you can lift the sender's prints."

"We'll do the best we can." The sheriff pulled on a glove, opened the paper bag and dropped the flag and the packaging inside. "Has there been any other reason to consider this a threat?"

Rico shook his head. "No, but a black Arabic flag, usually associated with ISIS, isn't something a friend sends another friend who has been through what Laurel Layne has."

"Agreed," the sheriff said. "You did the right thing to hand it over to us. We'll also notify Homeland Security and the FBI in case they know of any Islamic State elements in the area. I'm sure Jake is also tapping into his resources. He might have answers sooner than we will about factions in the area." The sheriff placed the paper bag of evidence in his vehicle, straightened and tipped his head toward the upstairs apartment. "How's Miss Layne?"

Rico's jaw tightened. "Holding up. But the flag shook her."

"Jake says you were on the team that extracted her and the two men who'd been captured by ISIS in Syria."

Rico nodded. "What those animals did to them was—"

"Inhuman." Sheriff Faulkner nodded. "Laurel was coming out of her shell since being home. Then that bastard buried her and Mallory Watts in drums. They almost died."

"There has to be something terribly wrong with someone who can be that cruel," Rico said.

"That's exactly right. Their brains have to be misfiring on some level." The sheriff gave Rico a chin lift. "Glad you're keeping an eye on Laurel. Our department is stretched thin. I could assign a unit to drive by and check on her periodically, but that might not be enough."

"I'm here," Rico assured him. "And I plan to stick to her like fly paper."

The sheriff's lips twitched. "She's a strong woman. Not sure she'll be happy to have someone following her around."

"She's already tried to get rid of me," Rico said. "I have thick skin. I'm not easily deterred."

"Good." The sheriff held out his hand. "Good to meet you, Rico. The Brotherhood Protectors are a great asset to this area. You've signed on with a great team."

"Nice to meet you, too," Rico said. "Thank you for your service."

The sheriff saluted. "And thank you for yours—especially for bringing Laurel back to us."

Rico watched as the sheriff drove away, feeling better about his choice to leave the Navy and join the Brotherhood Protectors. What he'd seen of Fool's

Gold and the residents made him glad he'd come to Colorado.

Now, if he could get his first assignment to accept him as her guardian angel, all his ducks would be in a row, and his job would be a little easier.

Fifteen minutes after Rico had left Laurel's apartment, the door opened.

Laurel appeared on the landing, wearing a white dress with a floral pattern in shades of pink and red. Her blond hair hung straight and thick, barely brushing her shoulders.

Rico remembered when she hadn't had any hair after ISIS had cut it all off. What a difference it made, framing her face.

After locking the apartment door, she stood at the top of the stairs for a moment.

Rico's heart stopped, frozen in time for a second of eternity. Then it remembered to beat, flooding his body with blood, adrenaline and something else.

Desire.

"Beautiful," he said aloud.

Laurel descended the steps one at a time, carefully placing her feet encased in red strappy stilettoes. When she reached the bottom, her brow puckered. She met his gaze while biting her bottom lip. "It's not too much?"

"Sweetheart, you look amazing," he said, his voice not much more than a whisper.

"This reunion isn't to celebrate getting together.

It's to commemorate one of our fallen comrades." She turned and started up the steps. "I'm going to change into jeans."

Rico grabbed her hand and halted her climb. "Don't," he said. "Did the people of your old unit see you when you returned from captivity?"

Her lips twisted. "Some of them came to see me at the hospital in Bethesda after they redeployed to the States."

"How were you then?" Rico asked.

"Not good," Laurel said. "I was suffering panic attacks and was afraid of every sound and of people touching me." She touched a hand to her hair. "My hair had grown an inch or two but looked awful. I still had scabs on my head and arms."

Rico met and held her gaze. "I remember how you looked when you came out of that hole." He shook his head. "You've come a long way since then. Why not let your unit know just how far you've come?"

Her brow puckered. "I don't know…"

"Change if it will make you feel better," he said softly. "But you're beautiful. You're alive, and you've overcome so much. Show them how far you've come."

She gave him a tremulous smile. "Mallory helped me pick out this dress to celebrate living through being buried alive. And she doesn't even like dressing up."

"It's a beautiful dress. But it's the woman wearing

it that makes it beautiful. Wear it, Laurel." He led her back down the steps and twirled her under his arm. "If you don't wear it...I will."

Laurel laughed out loud. "Now, that I'd like to see."

"You'd take me up on that?" He pressed a hand to his chest. "I'd lose face with my new boss. He might fire me."

"Relax," she said. "I'll wear it. But I'm still taking my own car. *And* I'm coming home alone." She raised her eyebrows. "Got a problem with that?"

"Not as long as you're wearing the dress, not me," he said with a wink. He held out his arm. "May I escort you to your car?"

She tipped her head back and stared down her nose at him. "You may." Her hand hooked his elbow, and she let him walk her to her car.

After inspecting the backseat through the window, he took her keys from her, unlocked the door and helped her into the driver's seat.

Laurel held out her hand.

He dropped the keys into her palm. "Want me to ride with you?"

She shook her head. "No, thank you. I'll get there on my own steam."

"As you wish." He closed the door and backed away.

Laurel started the engine and backed out of her parking space. With a little wave, she goosed the accelerator and sped away, leaving Rico scrambling to get to his truck.

He got caught at two of the lights on Main Street and didn't catch up to her until he broke the speed limits on the road out to Gunny's Watering Hole.

She pulled into the parking lot and found the last parking space near the far end of the paved parking.

Rico had to jump the curb and park in the grass. At least he was next to her when she got out of her vehicle and strode toward the front entrance of the bar. He hurried to catch up to her.

She stopped with her hand on the door. "If you don't mind...I'd prefer to go in on my own."

He backed a step. "By all means. I'll give you a head start."

"You don't even have to follow me in. Why don't you go to the lodge and get some rest? Don't forget, we start at four-thirty again tomorrow. I'll be fine here, surrounded by people from my old unit. I'm sure some of your fellow Brotherhood Protectors will be helping Gunny and RJ cook and serve."

This was his first assignment. He had to be with her to protect her, but she was blowing him off. Rico pressed a hand to his heart. "I'm crushed. I thought we'd established a connection."

"After a day of driving the van?" She shook her head. "You're delusional."

"Probably so," he said. "You'd deny me the pleasure of witnessing everyone's reaction to that dress?"

"Absolutely." She smoothed her hand over the skirt. "I'll tell you all about it tomorrow at four-thirty in the morning."

He'd give her some space, but not enough that she'd be out of his sight for long.

Trouble was brewing. He knew it in his gut. And that trouble was aiming for Laurel.

It was his job to protect her. He wasn't going to let anything happen to her on his watch.

So, he'd give her an inch but only an inch.

Laurel didn't know it yet, but she was his, whether she liked it or not.

That was...his responsibility.

CHAPTER 8

RICO STEPPED AWAY from the door, fully prepared to let her enter the bar alone.

Before she could open the door, a low-slung Mercedes sports car whipped into the parking lot and parked near the front entrance. There were no lines indicating a parking space.

The windows were tinted so dark Rico couldn't see the driver.

Rico stepped between the vehicle and Laurel.

The door opened, and Dr. Estep unfolded his long length from the driver's seat. When he spotted Laurel, he smiled. "Oh, good, I'm not terribly late. I was hoping I didn't have to go in alone. Do you mind if I join you?"

Laurel stepped around Rico. "Great timing, Dr. Estep. Rico was just going to the lodge. Would you do me the honor of escorting me inside?"

"It would be my pleasure." He held out his arm. "You look amazing in that dress. The guys won't recognize you."

"The last time I saw members of our unit, I was either wearing desert camouflage when we were in Syria or sweats and a T-shirt when I was in rehab." She grinned up at the doctor, making Rico's fists clench. "Shall we show them we are survivors?"

Dr. Estep smiled. "Yes."

As they pushed through the door of Gunny's Watering Hole, a cheer went up inside.

Rico stood outside, feeling like a balloon that had leaked out all its air.

He'd spent the entire day with Laurel Layne, only to be ditched as she'd walked into a redneck bar wearing that damned dress.

He wished he'd told her it was over the top for a place as casual as Gunny's. From the noise inside, the crowd that had gathered for the reunion, along with the cowboys fresh off the rodeo circuit, were happy to see a beautiful young woman in a pretty dress.

Rico waited forever, giving Laurel time to settle in with her old unit. When he looked at his watch, he realized he'd only stood outside for a full three minutes.

It had to be enough. After spending all day with Laurel, he couldn't wait to see her again.

Unfortunately, she didn't return the sentiment. Already, she'd tried to get rid of him several times.

Rico came from a long line of stubborn Hispanics from Mexico. His mother, a first-generation immigrant, had insisted her children learn to speak English. She'd refused to let them speak Spanish.

Rico might look like a Mexican with his dark hair, darker eyes and swarthy skin, but he barely spoke any Spanish. What he'd learned would have appalled his mother since it mainly consisted of curse words.

Rico entered the saloon and claimed a seat at the bar, not far from where people gathered around Laurel and Dr. Estep.

Laurel and Estep sat at a group of tables that had been pushed together to make more room for the members of Laurel's old unit.

Besides the men dressed in dusty jeans and even dustier cowboy hats, a few women hung on their arms and every word spoken. They shared narrow-eyed glares at Laurel, the female interloper, wearing a dress that was much more feminine than the jeans or denim skirts they wore with their scuffed cowboy boots.

Rico wished he'd told Laurel to change into the jeans she'd suggested, second-guessing her first choice of outfits to wear to the reunion.

She should have worn jeans and a T-shirt instead of the dress. The dress was out of place in the rustic bar. Which was the reason it had the attention of everyone in the bar—male and female.

Every man in the bar practically panted after her. The females wanted to scratch her eyes out.

Rico wanted to sweep Laurel up in his arms and carry her away where he could have her to himself.

That thought jolted him back to reality. He tried to tell himself that he wanted to isolate her to protect her. It was only half the truth. After spending most of one day with Laurel, he realized it wasn't enough. He didn't want to share her with anyone else.

That was a gut-punch moment.

Laurel was a beautiful woman with a personality to match. Everyone she touched walked away with a smile. Her flowers brought happiness to the receivers, and not just because they were beautiful, but because Laurel took the time to deliver them in person, taking a moment to make the receiver feel special, appreciated and loved.

This woman deserved the kind of joy and happiness she spread. Behind her smile was a shadow of fear. She'd been tortured by men who valued women less than they valued their cars, their male friends and their animals. They'd raped, beaten and confined her to a hole in the ground to rot. Alone. Scared. Hopeless.

Not only had she survived, but she'd also chosen to walk away from a career in health care to work with flowers. In bringing joy to others, she was finding delight in living despite the horrific events of her captivity in Syria and being attacked since she'd been home in Colorado.

Laurel deserved her happiness and freedom from fear.

Rico ordered a beer and watched the room out of the corner of his eye.

Laurel sat at a table, surrounded by men, each trying to buy her drinks. She smiled and spoke with each man, listening carefully and responding in a way that made the guy think he was the only man in the room.

Dr. Estep sat beside her, so close his knee touched hers. He draped an arm over the back of her chair as if staking a claim over her.

A primal urge made Rico want to knock the man's arm off the chair and pull him away from Laurel.

He clenched his fists and resisted, employing tension-release techniques he'd learned in therapy sessions for PTSD.

They helped a little, but he still wanted to knock the doctor's arm off Laurel's chair.

Several times during the first hour he sat at the bar, Rico caught Laurel looking his way. As quickly as she'd glanced at him, she turned away, directing her attention to something someone else said, turning her sweet smile on the man.

Rico's chest tightened every time she smiled at another man. Damn, he wished she was smiling at him.

Jake Cogburn entered the bar from the direction of the kitchen. When he spotted Rico, he weaved through the tables and slipped onto the stool beside him, turning to observe Laurel and the reunion of her unit. "How's it going?"

Rico shrugged. "They seem to be having a good time reconnecting."

"Laurel looks happy to see members of her old unit," Jake observed. "I got a little information from our computer guy, Swede."

Rico's attention turned to Jake, though he kept Laurel in his peripheral vision. "What did you find out?"

"Swede tapped his resources in Homeland Security and the FBI. There is an Islamic State faction hiding somewhere in the Colorado Rockies. Though why they'd choose to target Laurel Layne is a mystery, other than she was a survivor of ISIS torture."

"They couldn't pinpoint individuals in this faction?" Rico asked.

"It's an ongoing investigation. They're holding it close to their chests as they move in to shut them down. They hope to have good news soon."

Rico nodded. "The sooner the better."

"Swede also ran checks on Chris Monahan and Richard Estep."

Rico's brow rose. "And?"

"Their medical records indicate acute PTSD."

"That's no surprise," Rico said. "You should've seen them when we got them out of that shit hole in Syria."

"Monahan's symptoms were trouble sleeping, social isolation, chronic feelings of fear and anxiety, and…" Jake paused, "suicidal thoughts and behaviors."

"He just made good on his thoughts. I can tell you, when I have trouble sleeping because of PTSD, I sometimes wish I would just die and get it over with."

Jake nodded. "I fell into a bottle and tried to drink myself to death."

"How did you get past it?" Rico asked.

Jake's lip pulled upward on one corner. "The men of Brotherhood Protectors gave me no other choice —especially Joseph Kuntz and Hank Patterson. I wouldn't be here now if not for them yanking my sorry ass back into the real world. One thing they made me believe is that we're not done. I might not have the leg I was born with, but I can use my skills and training to help others. I've seen it again and again. If we don't step in to assist people who can't defend themselves or need someone who has their backs, those people could be dead. We're providing value. Saving lives. That's something worth living for."

As he nodded, Rico's gaze sought Laurel. "I agree. I just hope I don't fail that woman. She deserves a good, worry-free, happy life."

Jake tipped his head toward the group. "Richard Estep had some of the same PTSD symptoms, only he was also drinking heavily and displayed aggressive behavior, irritability and angry outbursts with the therapist and apparently with his wife. She divorced him after he slapped her face so hard it dislocated her jaw. He was drinking heavily at the time."

Rico was half out of his chair when Jake put a hand on his arm. "He's since had his license suspended and has been in therapy for anger management. He's taking drugs to calm his anger and anxiety. His therapist is pleased with his progress and thinks he has the aggression under control."

"Until he hits another woman," Rico gritted out between clenched teeth.

The waitress serving Laurel's table gathered empty glasses, took orders and returned to the bar.

Jake leaned toward her. "Hey JoJo, what's the doctor drinking?"

JoJo's brow dipped. "Which one's the doctor?"

"The tall, slim guy with the graying hair," Rico answered.

"Oh, him?" Her lips twisted. "He's on his third round of club soda. The others tried to talk him into tequila shots. He turned them down. Said he was one year sober and planned on staying that way."

Jake met Rico's gaze and shrugged.

"Just because he isn't drinking doesn't mean he isn't dangerous," Rico said.

The man in question excused himself from the others and headed for the bathroom.

"True," Jake said. "But what motive would he have to gift Laurel with an ISIS flag?"

"He, of all people, would know what effect it would have on her," Rico said.

Jake nodded. "What would he hope to accomplish by upsetting her?"

"I don't know. Maybe he's jealous that she has her life together and is happy and successful. Misery loves company?"

A few minutes later, the doctor rejoined the group but didn't take a seat. "I'm heading back to my hotel. Does anyone need a designated driver?"

The men all declined his offer.

"Then I'll see you tomorrow." The doctor left the bar.

"Looks like the party is breaking up," Jake said.

Laurel stood. "I have to be up early to open the shop, or I'd stay longer." She hugged each man, one at a time, her eyes shiny with tears. "It's good to see you all. I'll see you again tomorrow at the memorial." Her gaze shot to Rico.

He was already off his stool, ready to follow her. "Thanks for the info," he said to Jake.

He caught up to Laurel and passed her, reaching the door in time to open it for her.

"Thank you," she said.

"What?" He cocked an eyebrow. "You're not going to tell me you can open your own door?"

"Not tonight," she said, her tone subdued as she passed through the door and out into the night.

The Mercedes sports car that had been parked by the door was gone. "Dr. Estep didn't stay long," Rico noted.

"I didn't realize he was a recovering alcoholic when I arranged for us to meet at Gunny's." She crossed the parking lot slowly. "I should've kept up with him. I thought he was doing well." Laurel shook her head. "I'm not a very good friend if I don't check on the people I care about." She walked to the end of the parking lot and stopped to look up into Rico's gaze. "I wasn't looking forward to seeing everyone. I was afraid it would bring back too many bad memories." She smiled weakly, her eyes filling with tears. "But I'm glad I did. I have to stop being afraid of the past. And I need to keep in touch with people. I don't know if they're in trouble if I don't check on them every so often."

"Like Monahan?"

She nodded. "And maybe Dr. Estep. He looks like he's aged ten years since I last saw him."

Rico could have told her what he'd learned about the doctor, but the tears in Laurel's eyes kept him from making her more depressed. He could fill her in tomorrow on their delivery run.

She'd had enough drama for one day.

ELLE JAMES

Laurel fished in her purse for her keys. "Thank you for walking me to my car. I'm sorry if I haven't been very accepting of your kindness. I'm trying really hard to be my own person, to stand up for myself, and more importantly...to defend myself. I feel that if I accept your protection, I've failed myself."

He cupped her cheek. "Laurel, you haven't failed yourself. During BUD/S training, we learned to be strong as individuals but that we're stronger as a team. We look out for each other." He believed the words he said to his very core. It also reminded him that he'd failed his friend, Bert, to save this woman.

Laurel pressed her hand to the back of his and turned her cheek into his palm, pressing a kiss there. "Well, thank you for being a part of my team. But you don't have to follow me back to my apartment." She took a step backward. "I'll be okay. Besides, it would be out of your way since you're staying here at the lodge."

He didn't say anything. He'd follow her no matter what she said.

Her lips twisted. "You're going to follow me, anyway, aren't you?"

Again, he didn't say anything, but his lips twitched.

Laurel sighed. "You're a stubborn man."

"We have a lot in common."

She chuckled. "I guess so." Laurel turned toward

134

her car, stopped and tilted her head. "Is that tire flat?" She bent to examine her front left tire. "It is. Well, damn." She walked to the rear of the vehicle. "Good thing I know how to change a—flat." She stopped, pulled her cell phone out of her purse and switched on the flashlight, shining it down at the left rear tire.

Rico squatted beside the tire. "Two tires flat." He took her cell phone from her hand and circled the car. All four tires were flat. He got closer to one and studied it carefully.

"How could all four tires be flat at once?" Laurel said. "They're not that old."

He pointed to the tire in front of him, where a gash marred the sidewall. "These tires have been slashed." He straightened and looked around. He didn't know what he expected to find. It wasn't like the person who'd slashed Laurel's tires would stick around to be caught.

"What the hell?" Laurel pressed a hand to her mouth. "I'll have to call a tow truck. This means a whole new set of tires."

Rico handed Laurel's phone to her and pulled his out of his pocket along with the card Sheriff Faulkner had given him.

"Who are you calling?" Laurel asked.

"The sheriff. When I gave him the flag and the package it came in, we couldn't say for sure it was a threat. Slashing tires is an attack on your property.

Someone is out to get you or wants to make your life miserable." He hit send.

The sheriff answered on the first ring. "Sheriff Faulkner."

"Sheriff, Rico Cortez. We're at Gunny's Watering Hole. Laurel Layne's tires have all been slashed."

The sheriff muttered a curse. "I'm on my way."

Rico ended the call and texted Jake, telling him to step outside.

Then Rico glanced at Laurel.

She'd moved to the back of her vehicle, her eyes narrowing. Once again, she switched on her flashlight. This time, she didn't shine it down at the tires but at the back windshield.

Her hand shook, making the light bounce. "Wh... what's that?"

They'd been so focused on the tires that Rico hadn't noticed something had been drawn in black paint on Laurel's rear windshield.

It appeared to be a U with a dot in the middle. His gut clenched.

"What is it?" Laurel asked. "A symbol or something? What does it mean?"

Rico slid an arm around her waist. "I don't know. But I've seen it before. In Syria."

"Rico?" Jake's voice called out from the door of the bar.

Rico waved and shouted, "Over here!"

Jake jogged across the parking lot and stopped beside Laurel's car.

Rico tipped his head toward the wheels. "All four tires slashed. And this," he stepped aside so that Jake could get close enough to see the symbol on the windshield. "I've seen this before."

Jake's lips pressed together. "That's the Arabic symbol for Christian. ISIS used it to target Christian households for extermination."

Rico's heart dropped like lead to the pit of his belly.

Laurel leaned into him, her body trembling.

Jake turned to Laurel. "Like it or not, you need protection. You do understand that, right?"

Laurel nodded.

Jake tipped his head toward Rico. "I'm assigning Rico to provide that protection. Are you okay with that?"

Laurel stiffened for a moment and then sighed. "Yes."

"Good." Jake's eyes narrowed. "You're welcome to stay at the lodge until we figure this out."

Laurel shook her head. "My workday starts early enough without having to drive into town. I'll stay at my apartment."

Jake nodded. "Okay. The offer remains open if you change your mind."

"Thank you," Laurel said softly.

"After the sheriff has a look at the damage, I'll

have a tow truck drop your car at the tire shop in town."

"I can do that," Laurel said.

"I know you can," Jake said with a gentle smile. "But I can get a discount with the tow truck driver."

"I can't argue with that when I have to buy a whole new set of tires." Laurel gave Jake a twisted grin. "Thanks."

Jake walked a few steps away to place the call for a tow truck.

Laurel stayed where she was, staring at the symbol on her car. A shiver shook her body. "Why?"

"I wish I knew." Rico's arm tightened around her waist. "Sweetheart, get used to the idea that we're a team twenty-four-seven until we find this bastard."

CHAPTER 9

AFTER THE SHERIFF came and took their statements, Laurel didn't resist when Rico led her to his truck, opened the passenger door and handed her up into the seat. She was too tired to argue and too shaken to want to.

Though Laurel hated to admit it, having Rico there was a godsend. At this point, her choices were to accept his protection or move in with her brother and Mallory.

Devin and Mallory had just found each other again. Laurel didn't want to crowd them in their rekindled love. She wanted to live independently, but someone was making it difficult.

Rico's protection meant he'd be with her every hour of every day.

Her heart skipped several beats, and a swarm of butterflies erupted in her belly.

It wasn't as if she had a house with two or more bedrooms. Hell, she didn't even have a separate bedroom. Her apartment was fine for her alone. But having a man stay with her...in her apartment...

Her imagination raced ahead, inventing an entire scenario.

Rico would fill her apartment with his broad shoulders. He'd want to get a shower, which meant he'd have to get naked. Behind the bathroom door, of course. Just a few feet away from her bed.

While he was in the shower, she'd change out of her dress into something more suitable to sleep in.

He'd finish his shower and step out before she was fully dressed. He'd see her scars. Rico would know what they'd done to her. He'd be disgusted at the very thought of touching her. She'd be crushed and curl up in the fetal position and never be able to look him in the eye again.

No.

She wasn't ready.

Her pulse sped. By the time Rico parked at the rear of her shop, Laurel was in full panic mode.

She hadn't been alone with a man since...

Rico shut off the engine, climbed down from the truck and came around to open her door for her.

Laurel sat with her hands in her lap, staring at the building, not seeing it.

"Hey," Rico spoke softly. "Are you okay?"

Laurel pressed a hand to her chest, her breath arrested in her lungs. "I—I. Can't. Breathe."

"Oh, babe. Does it bother you that I'll be staying with you?" He shook his head. "I don't want to cause you even more stress. I just want to make sure you're safe." He ran a hand through his hair and looked up at her apartment door. "If it makes you feel better, I'll sleep on the landing outside your door. You'll have your apartment all to yourself."

Still, she couldn't move. Couldn't catch her breath.

"Hey, Laurel," he coaxed. "Look at me."

If he had touched her, she would have flinched. But he didn't. He stood a safe distance from her, giving her the space she needed without abandoning her.

"Look at me, Laurel," he insisted.

Slowly, she turned her head, her gaze connecting with his.

"Breathe," he whispered. "Like this." He drew in a deep breath.

He waited for her to follow suit.

Laurel focused on his words, on his motions and drew in a shaky breath.

"Now, let it out." He blew the breath out, stretching it out until all the air cleared his lungs.

Laurel released the breath she'd sucked in like he had. Slowly.

"Again," he said.

They repeated the process two more times.

By then, her pulse had slowed, and she no longer felt like she was suffocating.

He smiled. "Better?"

She nodded. "I'm sorry."

He shook his head. "Don't be. I know exactly how you feel. I learned that breathing technique in therapy. It's helped me through several panic attacks." He held out his hand. "Do you want help out of the truck, or do you want to do this on your own?"

"I'll do it on my own," she answered quickly.

Rico stepped back and let her climb out onto the running board. When she stepped down, she miscalculated the distance and pitched forward.

In a swift, fluid movement, Rico caught her.

His arms wrapped around her as she fell into his chest.

As quickly as he'd swept her up, he set her on her feet and stepped away with only a hand on her arm to make sure she could stand on her own.

"I shouldn't be allowed to wear high heels."

Rico chuckled. "Especially when riding in a truck."

Laurel nodded. "It was a little easier getting in and out of my car in these." She glanced at the stairs.

"You've got this," he whispered. "I'm only going up to clear the apartment before you go in. I'll step out as soon as I know it's safe."

She drew in a deep breath and let it out. Then she

squared her shoulders and walked carefully to the stairs, determined not to fall on her face. She wasn't acting like a woman who was capable of living on her own. Not when she was having a full-blown panic attack at the thought of having a man stay with her in her apartment. It wasn't like he was going to make love to her or anything.

Her imagination had blown everything out of proportion.

Rico was only there to protect her, not make love to her. Jake had assigned him to her like any other client.

Only Rico wasn't any other protector. He'd been the one to see her at her very worst. Beaten, shorn, naked and filthy from being abused by the animals who'd kept her captive.

So what if he saw her naked now? It couldn't be worse than when he'd first laid eyes on her.

He followed her up the stairs, close enough to catch her if she fell, but not touching her.

At the top of the stairs, he took her key from her, pulled his handgun from beneath his jacket and unlocked her door. "Are you going to stay here?"

She nodded.

Rico disappeared into her apartment.

For a full ten seconds, Laurel held her breath. The panic she thought she'd conquered reared up. All because she couldn't see Rico.

When he appeared in front of her, she let go of the air in her lungs with a woosh.

He frowned. "Forget to breathe again?"

She nodded.

He stepped aside. "Get in here," he said.

She crossed the threshold. As soon as she was in, he stepped out.

"I told you, I'll sleep out here on the landing. Your apartment is safe. I'll make sure no one gets in to hurt you." He pulled the door toward him.

Laurel grabbed the edge. "No. I wasn't panicking because you'd be in my apartment. I was panicking because I couldn't see you." She stared out at the landing. "If you're out here, I won't be able to see you."

His brow furrowed. "I thought you were panicking because you'd be alone with me in your apartment."

"I was, at first." She threw her hand in the air. "Then I wasn't. When you disappeared...I couldn't breathe." She stared at him in the light shining down on the landing. "What is wrong with me?"

He reached out as if to cup her cheek and stopped before his hand connected with her face.

She grabbed the hand before it dropped to his side and pulled him through the door into her apartment. "I'd rather be panicked with you inside my apartment than alone with you outside."

His gaze swept over her face. His forehead wrinkled. "Are you sure?"

"Positive." She smiled weakly. "See? I'm breathing." To prove the point, she inhaled deeply and released the air slowly.

"Just to be clear," he held up his hands, "I'm here to protect you. Not to molest you."

She sighed. "I know. I trust you."

"Thank you," he said, his tone sincere. "That means a lot."

She moved deeper into the apartment, which meant all of a few steps, and waved to the bathroom. "I had my shower earlier. You're welcome to it."

"I would like to rinse off." He grinned. "Who knew a man could work up a sweat delivering flowers?"

"It was an unusually warm day." She dropped down onto the couch just to move out of the way. "There are fresh towels on the shelf in the corner of the bathroom, shampoo and body wash in the shower itself. Help yourself."

"Thanks." He stared at her for a moment. "I have a gym bag in my truck with a change of clothes. Will you be all right while I go down to get it?"

"Sure. I'm feeling more like my normal, not crazy self," she said, thinking how lame she must sound. She pinched the bridge of her nose with one hand and waved the other. "Go. I'll be fine."

As soon as Rico stepped out the door and closed it behind him, Laurel was off the sofa.

She opened the door quietly and watched Rico as he hurried down the stairs, grabbed the bag out of the backseat of his pickup and headed back to the stairs.

Easing the door closed, she ran back to the couch and sat in the same spot she'd been when he'd left.

After a light tap, he opened the door and stepped inside with the gym bag. "Still okay?"

She nodded. "Great."

He closed the door, twisted the deadbolt and crossed to the bathroom. "I'll only be a few minutes."

"Take your time," she said, her voice sounding a little more breathless than she would have liked. "Although I have to warn you, it's a little water heater."

"I'll manage. Yell if you need me," he said, entering the tiny bathroom and closing the door behind him.

Laurel's heart fluttered. If she wasn't okay with a man in her apartment, she had a few minutes respite to get comfortable with the idea.

And to change out of the dress and into something comfortable to sleep in.

As soon as she heard the shower go on, she shot off the sofa, raced for her dresser and pulled out the faded, oversized T-shirt she wore every night to sleep in.

Laurel grimaced. It was about the least sexy thing she owned.

She tossed it back in the drawer and dug deeper

until she found the silky, smoky blue babydoll night-gown and matching bikini panties she'd purchased on a whim as a goal to strive toward. For that day when she finally worked up the courage to sleep with a man. That had been before she'd gone on her first date since Syria. That date being with Alan Croft, who'd tried to kill her and Mallory.

She stared at the beautiful nightgown and sighed. Who was she kidding? She'd just had a massive panic attack at the thought of getting naked with Rico.

If she actually got naked with the man, she'd be catatonic before he crossed the room. Getting nude with Rico wasn't an option anyway. He wouldn't make a move and risk triggering her panic. If she wanted him to touch her, she'd have to touch him first.

Her pulse quickened. This time, not in a panicky way. Instead, it quickened, spreading warmth through her body, that heat coiling around her core. Her breathing grew ragged at the thought of touching Rico's bare chest, her fingers skimming down those hard muscles and over his washboard abs.

Suddenly, she was hot, hot, hot, her body burning with the first flames of passion and desire she'd felt in a long time.

The water shut off in the bathroom.

Laurel's heart leapt. She shoved the nightgown to the bottom of the drawer, fighting back the raging desire taking her by storm. Making love with Rico Cortez couldn't happen. He'd see—

See what?

What he'd already seen.

Laurel stripped out of the dress and pulled the worn T-shirt over her head and down her body.

The bathroom door opened, and a rush of steam filled the apartment.

The air left Laurel's lungs.

Out of the steam, Rico emerged, carrying his jeans and shirt neatly stacked in his arms. He wasn't naked as he'd been in Laurel's imagination. He wore a T-shirt and gym shorts. A safe and uninspiring combination.

Or it should have been.

On Rico, it only served to emphasize the muscles that stretched the fabric tight across his chest and the thickness of his thighs peeking out of the hem of his shorts.

"Breathe, Laurel," he said, laying his clothes on the floor beside the sofa.

She drew in a breath and let it out. The technique helped deliver oxygen to her brain but did nothing to slow her pounding pulse.

He frowned. "Are you coming down with something?"

She blinked, processed his words and answered, "No. Why do you ask?"

"Your face is flushed." He closed the distance

between them and pressed a hand to her forehead. "You don't feel feverish."

Oh, yes, I do, she thought. *I'm burning up.*

His brow puckered. "Do you want me to make you a cool compress?"

She shook her head. "No, thank you." She wanted him to fan the flames and make her even hotter.

How had this happened? From panic attack to passion attack. Laurel was a hot mess.

"Sit down." Rico led her to the sofa. "I'll get you some water."

She sank onto the cushion, her body shaking with the force of her unexpected need.

"Where are your glasses?" he asked.

She only had four cabinets. Laurel almost laughed, but didn't, afraid she'd sound hysterical.

He opened and closed cabinet doors. "Never mind. I found them." Rico opened the small freezer and scooped ice into the glass, then filled the glass from the tap. A moment later, he sat on the sofa beside her and handed it to her.

She drank a sip, letting the cool liquid slide down her throat. Then she set the glass on the table and stared down at her hands in her lap.

"What's wrong?" Rico asked.

She shook her head. "I'm afraid," she admitted.

"Laurel, I'm here to protect you. I won't let anyone in to hurt you." He held out his hand. It was her choice whether she wanted to take it.

She laid her hand in his.

His fingers closed around hers, not so tightly that she couldn't escape, but enough that she could feel his strength.

"If it's me you're afraid of, I can park my ass out on the landing. I'll be close, but not in your space. It's up to you. The last thing I want to do is hurt you or make you afraid. Do what makes you comfortable."

"That's just it," she said, staring at their hands. "Nothing about you makes me feel comfortable."

CHAPTER 10

RICO STARTED to pull his hand away, his chest tight, heart heavy. "That's it. I'm leaving. The landing is fine. I've slept in worse places."

Laurel held onto his hand. "No. I want you to stay. I also want you to understand what I barely understand." She shook her head from side to side. "You make me feel things I never thought I'd feel again."

"Like what?" he asked. "Anger? Frustration? Impatience?" He'd named a few he was feeling.

She laughed, the sound short and sharp. "All of that and more." Laurel looked into his eyes. "You make me uncomfortable with passion and desire."

Stunned, he leaned back. "Okay, that's a surprise."

The flush in her cheeks deepened. "For you and me both."

His brow dipped. His pulse leaped at her admission at the same time as his gut clenched. "And that frightens you?"

She nodded.

"Babe, I'd never do anything to hurt you. Is that what you're afraid of?"

"No," she answered quickly. "And yes."

"Are you afraid I'll touch you?"

She bit her bottom lip and glanced down at their joined hands. "I'm afraid you won't."

He gave a short bark of laughter. This woman made his blood burn. "Why would you think I wouldn't? I've wanted to touch you since you ran into me on the path between the bar and the lodge."

She looked away. "You were the one who rescued me. You saw me at my very worst. You know what they did to me."

He squeezed her hand gently, the image of her naked, filthy and afraid like a knife twisting in his chest. "You didn't ask for it. You didn't deserve what happened. You have nothing to be ashamed of. Laurel, *you* were the victim. Any man who holds that against you isn't worthy of you."

She snorted. "I still feel violated, dirty and disgusting. No matter how many showers I've taken, the number of years that have passed or the blood tests that prove I don't have any sexually transmitted diseases, I'm tainted. I'm afraid to let a man touch me. Afraid he'll turn away in disgust. Afraid his touch will trigger a panic attack. Afraid my scars will be too much of a reminder of what they did. Or even worse, I'm afraid he'll only make love to me because he pities me."

Her fears tore at his heart. "Oh, babe," Rico said. "You are a mess."

She stared at him, her brow puckering. "You're not supposed to agree with me."

"Why not?" He opened his arms. "You're afraid. So am I."

"You?" Her eyes narrowed. "That's not possible. You carried me out of that ISIS compound with bullets flying all around us. Even after you were hit, you kept going. You're my hero. The man who risked his own life to save me."

Memories of that night still haunted him. Not of how dirty she'd been, but of how he'd failed Bert. "I'm no hero. I did my job. And I lost a friend in the process."

Laurel's gaze met his, her eyes filling. "The member of your team who didn't make it. I'm so sorry."

"That night shook my confidence and stripped away the shreds of any superhero cape I might have mistakenly worn." He turned her hand over in his and traced her lifelines. "I'm afraid that no matter how hard I try, I won't be smart enough, strong enough or fast enough at the exact moment I need to be to keep that from happening again."

"You're afraid you can't keep me alive?" She shook

her head. "If this guy gets to me and I die, it won't be because you didn't do your best."

"Right." His chest was so tight he pressed his hand to the center and rubbed the muscles, hoping to relieve the strain. "I'm afraid my best won't be good enough."

She held his hand in hers. "We're a team. We look out for each other and for ourselves. You're not totally responsible for my well-being." Laurel frowned. "And what's all this talk about dying? It's bringing me down. Hard."

"I've only begun telling you what I'm afraid of," Rico said. "Do you want to hear more?" Maybe if she knew the extent of his fears, she'd turn and walk away. Then he wouldn't be holding her hand, and his body wouldn't be on high alert in anticipation of her acting on her passion and desire.

"No. Not when I'm on fire with desire." She lifted his hand to her face. "That's not fever from the flu. It's fever from me imagining you naked." Her lips pressed together. "At least it *was* heat from desire. You really know how to throw water on the flame."

"Sweetheart, I'm not sure you're ready for this. Not after that panic attack in my truck."

"Maybe you're right." She sat back against the couch. "At least answer this…" She met his gaze. "If I *was* ready, and knowing what you know about me, would you be willing?"

His mouth spread in a wide grin. "Do bees love

honey? Do pigs love mud? Do bears shit in the woods?" Rico raised a hand to the heavens. Could she not see that he was attracted to her? "Hell, yes."

"Really?" She rolled her eyes even as her chest swelled at his enthusiastic response. "Do bears shit in the woods? That's the best analogy you could come up with?"

"Well, they do, don't they?" His smile broadened. "And the answer is *yes*. That's what counts, right?"

"How do we know this isn't the right time for me to get back on the horse and ride?"

Rico raised a challenging brow. "Who's using bad analogies now? Am I a horse? Although I'd like to think a certain part of me is." He winked.

Laurel lifted her chin. "I'm ready." She drew a deep breath and let it out like he'd shown her earlier. "See? I'm breathing fine now."

His smile slid into a frown. "What happens if something triggers your panic in the middle of…you know?"

"In the middle of making love?" Laurel shrugged. "I'll use your breathing exercise until I get over it."

"I don't know. When you think about it, maybe we aren't right together. I've got my own issues with PTSD. You need someone who isn't going to wake up swinging."

"Who says I haven't woken up swinging?" Laurel asked.

"Ha! My point exactly," he said. "We're two broken people. We could kill each other in our sleep."

"I'm not asking for forever. I just want to know if I'm ready to move past the anxiety that has crippled me sexually for the past three years."

"Sweetheart, we might not even be sexually compatible." Rico didn't believe for a minute they weren't sexually compatible., but he had to make her think through this decision.

"I find you attractive. My body responds to yours without even touching." She frowned. "You said you'd be willing. Did you say that because you mean that? Or just to make me feel better about myself?"

He brushed his finger along her cheek, liking how smooth and silky it was. "Laurel, you are a beautiful woman. I'm attracted to you. I'm fighting a losing battle, trying not to take advantage of you when you're so vulnerable. You're asking me to make love to you just to see if you can? And if we fail to leave each other satisfied, will we consider this experiment a failure? Hell, we haven't even kissed."

Laurel trapped his cheeks between her hands and pressed her lips to his.

He tried to remain stoic and unfazed. God, it was hard with her warm, soft body brushing against his.

Leaning closer, Laurel pressed her breasts against his chest and deepened the kiss, skimming her tongue across the seam of his lips.

When he opened to her, she thrust past his teeth and caressed his tongue with hers.

The tight rein Rico had on his control evaporated. His stiff body melted against hers. His arms came up around her, pressing her closer, ever so gently.

Laurel straddled his hips and rubbed her sex across his hardening crotch.

Rico moaned into her mouth and broke the kiss. "Do you know what you're doing?"

"I have a good idea." She ran her hands through his hair and down the sides of his face to tug on his beard. "I've never made love to a man with a beard," she admitted.

"I can shave it," he offered.

"No way. It's that part of you that makes you even more interesting. Kissing you is warm and fuzzy."

His laughter caught on an indrawn breath as her hands slipped beneath his shirt.

He captured her hands in his. "Anything that happens here will be with you leading. I don't want you to feel trapped or forced in any way."

Her mouth returned to his in a mind-numbing kiss that made his entire body come alive with possibilities.

"Thank you," she whispered against his lips. Then she pushed his shirt up his torso, her fingers splaying across his skin.

He grasped the fabric and ripped it over his head.

When she reached for the hem of her T-shirt, he

refused to help. "Don't take it off if it makes you uncomfortable."

Laurel hesitated. She leaned over him and switched off the single lamp on the table beside him, plunging them into darkness. The only light came from the streetlight shining around the edges of the curtains in the windows.

He'd seen her body naked and dirty, but she obviously wasn't ready for him to see her bare skin, scarred by the beatings and the burns. If she wasn't ready for one thing, it was to bare her ugliness to this man. The night was an experiment to see if she could make love without losing her shit to a panic attack, reliving the torture she'd endured in that hell hole.

Under the cloak of darkness, Laurel slipped her T-shirt over her head and laid it on the end table, within easy reach.

Laurel leaned into him, pressing her breasts against his chest, loving the way his coarse curls tickled her sensitive nipples. She was grateful he couldn't see the scars where she'd been bitten and burned on her breasts and along her inner thighs. "Darkness is a great equalizer."

Rico lightly ran his hands up her sides to cup her breasts. "I'd rather see you in the light. All of you."

"I'm not ready for that." Laurel feathered her fingers through the hairs on his chest, searching for and finding the tight brown nipples. She pinched them lightly and then bent to take one into her mouth, rolling it gently between her teeth.

His hips rose automatically beneath her, his cock tenting his jogging shorts, pressing against the fabric of her panties.

Rico's breath hitched as a wave of intense longing washed over him. He wanted to be inside her so badly it physically hurt to hold back, but she was afraid.

What if it triggered those painful memories her mind had mercifully blocked? What if she could never have a man inside her again without remembering how those animals had raped her.

Rico didn't want to be the man who brought those memories back to her. He didn't want to be the cause of resurfacing the terror and pain.

"I've spent the last three years rebuilding my confidence, conquering my fears and taking charge of my life," Laurel said. "If we do this, it's another extension of my recovery."

She raised his hand to her lips and pressed a kiss to his fingertips. "I want this. I need to be filled with tenderness and raw, beautiful passion, not hate, regret and shame."

Laurel slid off his lap, held out her hand and pulled him to his feet.

Still, Rico hesitated. "Is this where you tell me never mind?" he asked. "Because if it is, I'll need to take another shower."

"No. This is where we take it to the bed." Still holding his hand, she led him the few steps across the floor without bumping into anything. "I'm getting too old and stiff to wrestle you on the sofa."

"Old, huh?" He chuckled. "Are you even thirty yet?"

"Thirty-three."

"Ancient," he pronounced. "Hold on." He bent to retrieve his jeans and fished out his wallet and the packet within. "Got it."

"Got what?" she asked.

Rico held up a packet barely visible in the limited lighting. "Consider it the protector's protection."

Laurel smiled. "Glad you're thinking ahead."

"Always prepared." He tossed the condom onto the nightstand and gathered Laurel loosely in his arms.

"I'm not made of glass," Laurel said. "You're not going to break me if you hold me a little tighter."

His hold tightened just a bit. "The first sign of panic, let me know. I'll let go and step aside."

Laurel nodded. "Just don't jump the gun. I'll tell you if I need you to back off."

"Aye, aye," he said, saluting her.

Laurel backed him up to the bed until the backs of his knees bumped into the mattress.

Planting her fingers against Rico's chest, she gave a gentle shove.

Rico sat on the bed. His boner jutted upward, forming a tent in his shorts.

Laurel hooked the elastic waistband of his shorts and met his gaze. "Am I moving too fast?"

He chuckled. "That's my line."

"Not today," she tugged his waistband downward. "Yes or no?"

"Yes."

She dragged his shorts over his hips, legs and ankles until they cleared his feet. She tossed the shorts over her shoulder and smiled. "Commando."

"Lucky coincidence. I didn't have a spare pair in the gym bag."

"What's your preference, boxers or briefs?" she asked.

"Boxer briefs," he answered. "Or nothing at all."

Her gaze rested on the evidence of his own desire, a rock-hard erection jutting straight out.

His dick responded to her perusal by swelling even tighter.

Laurel's tongue swept across her lips.

Nothing stood between them but the lace of her panties.

Laurel stood, shimmied out of her panties and tossed them aside.

The defining moment had arrived. Could she do it?

Would driving his hard cock deep inside her only drive her away in terror?

"If you're uncertain, let me help you make up your mind."

She frowned down at him, her expression unreadable in the murky darkness. "Okay. What do I do?"

Rico scooted back onto the bed, lying on his back. "Now you climb onto the bed."

On all fours, she crawled onto the mattress beside him.

"Turn around on your hands and knees," he said.

She did as he instructed.

He lifted her knee closest to his head and ducked his head beneath her hips. His hands splayed across her buttocks, easing her down over his mouth. He parted her folds and flicked her clit with the tip of his tongue.

Laurel gasped.

"Do you like that?" he asked.

"Yes," Laurel said, sinking her hips lower over his face.

He flicked her again.

A moan rose in her throat.

Rico chuckled, gripped her ass and showed her how good it could be on top.

He swirled his tongue around her clit until she writhed to the rhythm he set.

While his tongue played her most sensitive point, he slid a single digit into her moist channel.

Laurel stiffened.

"Breathe," he whispered.

She drew in a deep breath and let it out.

"Want me to back out?" he asked.

Soon, the combination of his tongue on her clit and his fingers inside her had her rocking, moaning and so wet.

Rico teetered on the edge of an orgasm without penetrating her, imagining how good it would feel to be inside her.

She stiffened, cried out and held her breath as her hips rocked with her release.

When she finally moved, Rico was so hard he was sure he'd have blue balls that night if he didn't have a release of his own.

But he wasn't going to assume she wanted him that way. She'd have to come to him.

Laurel dragged in a shaky breath, let it out and turned her body around to kiss him. "I didn't think I could ever feel that way again. That was amazing."

He grinned. "I aim to please," he said. "Ready to sleep?"

She stared down into his eyes. "Are you?"

"Sweetheart, you're calling the shots here."

"As good as that was…" she trailed a hand over his chest and down his ribcage, "I don't feel like it was… enough." Her hand encircled his cock. "I want more."

He stared at her long and hard. "Don't do this because you think I need it." Which he did, but that wasn't the point.

"I want you, Rico," she said, her hand tightening around his shaft. "All of you." That hand slid to the base and fondled his balls. "Inside me." Her eyebrows formed a V he could just see in the darkness. "And don't ask me if I'm sure. I wouldn't be lying naked with you if I wasn't. I knew where I wanted this to go. Now, if *you're* not sure…we can stop here." She released his cock. "Are you all in?"

Rico groaned. "Woman. That's what I'm supposed to say. If you don't know that I'm all in by now, I don't know how else to prove it to you."

Her smile flashed in the darkness.

"On one condition," he added.

The smile disappeared. "Sweet Jesus. Make it an easy one. I'm still so hot I might combust. Name it. What's the condition?"

"You're on top."

"Done." She leaned across him, her breasts brushing across his chest. After patting the surface of the nightstand for a couple of seconds, she said, "Got it." Laurel sat up in the bed, tore open the packet and rolled the condom over his rock-hard erection.

Her hands smoothing over his cock made him thrust upward.

He was so ready he might not last any longer than a teenage boy on a hot date.

Laurel rose on her knees, straddled his hips and, with her hand, guided his dick to her entrance.

With the tip of his cock engaged, she released it

and paused for a long moment. Long enough to worry Rico.

"Laurel?"

"Shush," she whispered. "I didn't think it would be this hard."

He knew she wasn't talking about his erection. Rico gripped her hips, ready to lift her off him and end the experiment.

"No." Her hands rested on his. "I'm okay. I just need to ease into this. The last time..." she choked on what sounded like a sob.

The last time someone had been inside her she had felt nothing but pain, terror and humiliation.

"You're not ready." His hold tightened on her hips.

"No. Really. I...need this." As she said the words, she lowered herself slowly, taking him in. Her channel tightened around him.

He was at once turned on and hesitant.

Laurel had been through so much.

Rico didn't want to compound her trauma by being too forceful or eager.

It took every ounce of his control to hold back when all he wanted to do was flip her onto her back and thrust deep inside her.

And yet, as excruciatingly slow as she came down on him, he experienced every minute nuance of her body accepting him. Her moist warmth wrapped around him. The tightness of her channel took him to the next level in a slow journey he would remember for the rest of his days.

By the time Laurel was firmly seated on his groin, Rico was holding his breath, straining to retain control of his baser instincts.

Laurel's breathing was erratic as if she alternated between breathing and gasping.

"Laurel?" he whispered.

"I'm okay," she said. "It feels…good. Better than I expected."

Rico let go of the air in his lungs and chuckled. "What did you expect it to feel like?"

"I expected pain," she said softly.

His heart squeezed hard in his chest. He wished he could take away that pain and suffering she'd experienced.

Her smile flashed in the gloom. "I felt no pain, Rico. In fact, it feels pretty amazing."

His pulse leaped, and his cock jerked inside her.

Laurel laughed. "I felt that." She rose on her knees.

He slid out all the way to the tip before she reversed directions and came down on him again.

"Mmm," she moaned. "Yes. Pretty damned amazing."

About to come apart at the seams, Rico held on by a thread as Laurel rocked up and down, her channel clenching around him, warm, wet and so incredibly wonderful.

She increased her speed, moving faster and faster.

Rico tensed, holding out until he couldn't stand it anymore.

Laurel rose again, all the way up and off.

He gasped. The shock of her pulling away delayed his release. "Are you done?" he asked, his voice strained between his teeth.

"Oh no. I'm just tired of doing all the work. It's your turn." She rolled onto her back. "Hopefully, we satisfied your condition." She spread her legs, her hand sliding down her belly to the juncture of her thighs. "That is, unless you've had enough?"

"I don't think I could ever have enough of you." Rico eased over her, careful not to rest his weight on her body. He didn't want her to feel trapped, restrained or unable to escape at any moment. He settled his knees between her thighs, his hands planted on either side of her shoulders, his cock nudging her slick entrance. "You'll tell me if it's all too much?"

"Oh, for the love of—yes!" she said, the words coming fast, breathless. "Rico, I'm so close. Stop talking and make love to me, already." Her hands rose to grip his hips, her fingers digging into his buttocks.

She brought him all the way home, hard and swift.

"Slow down," he whispered. "I don't want to hurt you."

"I'm so close." She writhed beneath him. Her heels came up and dug into the mattress.

He eased out. When he slid back in, she rose to meet him.

"Faster," she urged.

The passion in her voice severed the last of Rico's control. He thrust into her again and again, his hearing tuned in should she feel overwhelmed. Her hands on his hips gave him all the information he needed.

Laurel wanted to ride this to the end. Her body tensed. She raised her hips and called out. "Now."

Already at the edge, Rico's release blasted through him, the sensations so intense, his body shook, his cock pulsed, and he drove deep inside her.

For a long moment, he held still. Then he moved in and out, slowing the pace until Laurel fell back against the mattress, her knees lowering.

She lay so still, it scared Rico.

"Laurel?"

"Mmm," she murmured.

"Are you—"

She reached up and pressed a finger to his lips. "Don't. I'm okay." Her smile flashed white in the gloom. "I'm so okay I could go for round two."

He chuckled, pulled free and dropped to the mattress beside her.

She moved closer, settling into the crook of his arm, laying an arm over his chest, her calf over his thigh. "Round two..." she yawned, "coming up...just as soon as I've rested my eyes for a minute."

He kissed the top of her head and held her close, but not too tightly, as she slipped into a deep sleep.

Rico lay for a long time, wrestling with what had just happened between them.

On the one hand, he was happy for Laurel. She'd taken a huge step in her recovery by allowing a man to make love to her.

Oh, and how great it had been. Her body fit perfectly with his; their chemistry was off the charts.

But she had a long way to go to feel good about herself. She'd turned out the lights so he wouldn't see her scars.

He'd felt the ridges of the scars across her back and the round burn marks on her breasts where her captors had pressed lit cigarettes into her skin.

She'd admitted to feeling unclean and unworthy because her captors had raped her over and over.

A good man wouldn't see that in her. He'd see the beautiful, kind woman who dedicated her days to bringing happiness to others through her flowers. He'd see her as beautiful inside and out. The past was in the past. Terrible things had happened, shaping her into the person she was today. She needed a patient, gentle man who would stand by her as she worked through her issues.

Hell, Rico had enough of his own issues. He wasn't sure he was the man she needed. He might compound her problems with his own.

For a long time, he held her, his fingers tracing

the scars. He wanted to kiss every one of them. He wanted to take away her pain, her fear and the crazy man determined to stir up her painful past.

As much as he wanted to stay with her, Rico didn't trust himself. He didn't have control of his dreams. Sometimes, he woke himself swinging at the enemies attacking him or Bert in his nightmares. He couldn't risk falling asleep with Laurel.

He rose from the bed, tucked the sheets and blankets around Laurel's naked body and stared at her for a moment, wishing for so much more. Then he stretched out on the sofa, his feet dangling over the arms. For a long time, he lay awake, going over all that had happened in such a short amount of time. Fear swelled inside him. He was afraid for Laurel's life. He was afraid that he wouldn't be able to protect her.

Most of all, he was afraid he was falling in love with this beautiful woman who deserved a better man than him. Afraid that when they caught her tormentor, he wouldn't be able to walk away with his heart intact.

CHAPTER 11

LAUREL WOKE in the dark hours of the morning. She didn't wake because of a nightmare but because she'd heard a sound. She blinked her eyes open and listened, trying to pinpoint the origin.

When she stretched out an arm, she expected to find Rico lying in the bed beside her. The space was empty; the sheets were cold.

Laurel sat up, pulling the sheet up over her breasts, shivering in the cool night air.

A low moan rose from across the room.

Her pulse quickened. She tossed aside the sheets, swung her legs over the side of the bed and pushed to her feet. She'd only taken a step when her toes encountered soft fabric.

Reaching down, she lifted a T-shirt off the floor, held it to her nose and smiled. It smelled of aftershave and the outdoors.

Rico.

Laurel slipped the shirt over her head and padded barefoot across the floor to the sofa.

Rico lay sprawled across the cushions, his feet hanging over the arms.

Laurel frowned.

Why had he chosen to sleep here when they'd already gotten naked together and made love? Was he positioning himself between her and the door to stop anyone from getting to her?

Silly man. That's what locks were made for.

Or was he distancing himself from her, letting her know what had happened between them was a one-night-stand, and he didn't plan on a repeat performance?

Her heart sank. Had she been that bad?

He'd seemed to enjoy making love to her. Or was that wishful thinking?

Rico mumbled something unintelligible, flinched and slung his arm over his face. His legs jerked, and his body twisted.

In the limited lighting, Laurel could see his dark brows forming a V over his nose.

"No," he muttered. "No," he said louder.

The man was in trouble in his dreams.

Laurel couldn't stand there and watch him suffer. She leaned over him and touched his shoulder. "Rico."

He turned over, knocking her hand away, his distress increasing.

"Rico," Laurel spoke louder. "Babe, wake up. You're having a bad dream."

His head moved side to side, and his hands bunched into fists. He ducked his head as if avoiding a hit.

Laurel touched his shoulder again. "Rico."

Caught in his dream, Rico didn't hear her. He was lost in a fight, desperately defending himself.

With her heart hurting for him, Laurel placed both hands on his shoulders and shook him. "Rico, wake up!"

His arms came up, knocking her hands away from his shoulder, and he swung a fist, connecting with her jaw.

Laurel let out a startled screech and staggered backward, tripping over the shoes she'd left on the floor the night before. She landed flat on her back; the air knocked from her lungs.

"Laurel!" Rico was up off the couch in a heartbeat. "Laurel!" He fumbled for the switch on the table lamp, found it and flooded the room with light.

"Oh my God." He dropped to his knees beside her. "Did I do this?"

She struggled for air.

Rico slipped a hand beneath her shoulders and helped her to a sitting position. "Breathe, Laurel. Breathe.

She sucked in a ragged breath and blew it out.

"Oh, babe, I'm sorry," he sat on the floor and pulled her into his lap. "The dreams get hold of me... I'm sorry." He leaned her back and stared into her face. "Where did I hit you? Where does it hurt?"

Finally able to speak, she cupped his cheek. "I'm fine."

He frowned down at her. "No, you're not." He brushed his thumb across her jaw, barely touching her.

Laurel winced.

"You have a bruise there," he said, his lips thinning. "I did that to you."

"It was my fault. I shouldn't have tried to wake you from the dream."

He pulled her close and held her for a long moment, resting his cheek against her hair. When he lifted his head, he stared down at her, his face serious, resolute. "I'll let Jake know he'll need to find someone else to protect you."

"No." Laurel laced her hands behind his head. "I don't want someone else. I want you."

"I stepped over the line. I never should've made love to you." Rico shifted her out of his lap and rose to his feet. Then he held out a hand and helped her to her feet.

"I wanted you to. I want you to make love with me again." She rested a hand on his chest.

His brow creased heavily as he stared at her jaw. "I hit you."

"No, you hit the enemy in your dream. I just happened to be in the way." She smiled up at him.

He set her away from him, paced to the door and turned to face her. "You're the client. I'm supposed to protect you, not cause you injury."

She closed the distance between them. "It was my fault. I shouldn't have tried to wake you."

He shoved a hand through his hair. "Laurel, you've been through so much. I don't need to add to your trauma. It would be best if I stepped out of the picture and let Jake assign someone who won't punch the client."

"Stop it," Laurel spoke firmly. "I know where you're coming from. I'm the same. I have nightmares where I come up swinging. I knocked over a lamp one night."

"Knocking over a lamp isn't the same as punching a woman." His gaze fixed on the bruise on her jaw, and he shook his head. "You deserve someone you can trust not to hurt you. I'm no good for you."

She took his hand and pressed it to her cheek. "You're the best thing that's happened to me in a long time. I couldn't have done what I did last night without your patience and understanding. For me, last night was not only a breakthrough but incredibly special. I didn't want it to end." She pressed a kiss into his palm. "I still don't want it to end," she said softly.

His fingers pressed against her skin for a moment. Then he pulled his hand free of hers. "The risk is too great. I can't be with you." He nodded toward her bed. "Go to sleep, Laurel. Four o'clock will be here all too soon." His tone wasn't commanding but rather more resigned and maybe sad.

"What about you?" she asked. "You need sleep."

He gathered his clothes, the gym bag and shoes and headed for the door. "I'll be on the landing where I should've stayed to begin with."

"You can't sleep on the landing," Laurel insisted.

"You're right. I'll be awake, guarding your door, doing what I'm being paid to do." He pulled the door open and started through it.

Laurel's heart pounded, and her pulse raced. "Rico. Stay with me," she said. "I won't ask you to make love to me again. You can sleep on the sofa. I'll stay in my bed. If you have a nightmare, I won't try to wake you." She smiled weakly. "Promise."

He shook his head. "I need to clear my head." Then he paused and glanced back at her. "You're not having a panic attack, are you?"

"Would you stay if I was?" she asked.

"You know I would," he said.

Laurel wanted him to stay because he wanted to be with her, not because he felt sorry for her. She lifted her chin, willing her pulse to slow and her heart to quit racing. "No. I'm not having a panic attack," she lied.

He stared at her a moment longer as if he didn't quite believe her. Finally, he stepped across the threshold and turned. "I'll be on the other side of this door if you need me." The door closed.

Laurel's heart raced so fast that she grew light-headed. Rather than pass out on the floor, she staggered to the sofa and sat, pressing a hand to her chest.

"Breathe, Laurel," she whispered, remembering how those words had sounded coming from Rico. Something in his tone and the way he'd spoken had calmed her when her mind and body spun out of control.

He wasn't there this time to talk her down, to remind her to breathe.

For several long minutes, Laurel felt like she was having a heart attack. But she'd die rather than ask Rico to help. He wanted nothing to do with her, convinced he wasn't right for her. He'd hurt her. The bruise on her jaw was nothing compared to the rip in her heart.

Hell, maybe a heart attack was what she needed to end the insanity, to still the panic attacks and erase her need to be loved and desired. For a brief time, she'd dared to hope she could have a normal life with a man who saw her for the person inside, not the scars on the outside.

She suffered through the panic attack alone, as she had for the past three years. Eventually, her heart rate slowed, and her pulse returned to normal. By then, she was so weak she laid over on the sofa and curled into the fetal position. Holding her knees to her chest, she let the tears flow.

At some point, she must have fallen asleep. The shrill ringing of her alarm jerked her awake. She staggered across the room, slapped the alarm into silence and stared at the bed with its disturbed sheets and blankets. There was still an indentation on the pillow where Rico had rested his head after making love to her. Had it only been a few hours ago?

It felt like a lifetime had passed.

Though she didn't want to face the day, she had a business to run, people to please and a memorial to attend before she could return to her little apartment and solitary bed.

Despite a heavy heart, her day began like every other day. The same old routine. Get dressed. Brush her teeth. Pull her hair back into a ponytail and go downstairs to the shop.

Only this time, Rico would be waiting on the landing to escort her into her shop to ensure her safety. Her chest tightened as she remembered how beautiful it had been making love with him after years of telling herself she was damaged goods and unworthy of sharing her body with a man.

Too bad what had started so wonderfully had ended so soon.

To bolster her flagging confidence, she chose to wear a pretty white sundress with a yellow and white daisy pattern. It cheered her up every time she wore it.

She spent more time than usual with her makeup, stalling more than improving her appearance and using concealer to hide the bruise. As much as she wanted to see the man, she wasn't looking forward to facing Rico.

She didn't know how she was supposed to act in front of Rico. They'd been naked together less than twelve hours earlier. Was she supposed to be embarrassed, shy, humiliated or angry?

She was a little bit of all those emotions, but mostly, she was sad. But what could she do to make it easier?

Like she'd faced every day of her recovery, she squared her shoulders and powered through. She was a survivor.

He was there when she opened the door, standing on the landing with his back to her, staring into the darkness.

"Good morning," she said softly, the still of the early hour making her feel like she should whisper.

He turned, the light shining down on his stony

face. Were those shadows beneath his eyes? Were the crow's feet at the corners of his eyes a little more pronounced?

"You look tired," she said. "Why don't you take a day off and get some rest?"

"I will once Jake finds a replacement for me," he said.

"Still going with that theory?" Laurel sighed. "Am I that bad to be around?"

"No." He closed his eyes briefly, his lips pressing into a thin, hard line. "You're that good." He turned and walked down the steps in front of her.

Laurel stood on the landing, studying his stiff back and stoic countenance. He appeared tense, like he'd been when he'd fought that battle in his dreams. Was that it? Was he fighting an internal battle against himself?

Her heart dared to lighten.

You're that good echoed in her head.

The man wanted her.

He had some PTSD issues.

So did she.

Who would understand them better than each other?

They had chemistry. She enjoyed his company. He seemed to enjoy hers. The one sticking point was his violent dreams.

She could live with that. As a team, they could work through it or find a workaround. She was open to the possibilities. The challenge was to get Rico to be equally open. What she needed was more time with the man.

As soon as she got a free moment, she'd call her friend, RJ, and put a bug in her ear that Rico might ask to be replaced. Laurel didn't want a different protector. Only Rico would do. RJ was her friend and had been after her to get back on that dating horse. She'd make sure Jake didn't have another guy to take over anytime soon.

With more time, Laurel could rev up the chemistry between her and Rico and make him fall so deeply in love with her that he'd move heaven and earth to be with her, even if it meant sleeping with his wrists tied to the bedposts.

Laurel's core heated at the thought. She'd never delved into kinky sex, but the new, take-charge-survivor-Laurel was open to the damned possibilities.

"Are you coming?" Rico asked from the bottom of the stairs.

Was she coming?

She met his gaze with a lift of her chin.

Hell yes, she was coming.

The question was, was he ready?

Laurel doubted it.

She wasn't just a survivor…she was a warrior about to fight for what she wanted.

And she wanted Rico.

She pasted a smile on her face and cranked up the wattage as she descended the steps and floated past Rico. "It's going to be a beautiful day. Can you feel it?"

He grumbled something beneath his breath that sounded like *goddamn morning people*, then turned to follow her.

When she reached out to unlock the back door to the shop, he took the key from her.

Dutifully, and with a bright smile, she stepped away from the door and waited for him to unlock, enter and search the shop for bad guys. She stayed put, counting the seconds, fighting the urge to march inside and get right to work.

Moments later, Rico appeared. "All clear."

Rather than shoot a snarky comment, she sailed past him, blessing him with another perky smile. "Thank you," she said and batted her eyelashes.

His brow sank low on his forehead, and his eyes narrowed. He didn't say anything, but he looked like he wanted to.

Laurel worked through her orders, making sure to need some item right behind anywhere Rico was standing. It didn't matter where he moved; she found an excuse to go to that location. When she got close enough, she'd reach around him, brush a breast against his arm, or graze his hip with hers.

If he was at all attracted to her, she wasn't going to let him forget. If he wasn't, well then, she'd gain some satisfaction out of annoying the hell out of him. Win-win, either way.

They loaded the van together, at one point bumping shoulders. Rico nearly dropped the vase he'd been carrying.

Laurel rescued the vase, making certain her fingers touched his in the process. He quickly backed away and nearly ran into Carissa, who'd just arrived for work, carrying a cup of coffee.

"Whoa there, tiger," she said. "I don't mind when you bump into me. In fact, I might even get off on it." She waggled her eyebrows suggestively. "But careful with the coffee. It's the equivalent of lifeblood."

"Good morning, Carissa," Rico said.

"Morning, gorgeous," she said.

Laurel turned from the rear of the van and smiled brightly at her assistant. "Isn't it a beautiful day?"

Carissa held up a hand in front of her eyes. "Hey, boss lady, can you turn down the volume? You're blinding me."

Laurel laughed. "By the time you drink that coffee, I'm sure you'll agree."

"Don't bet money on it." Carissa shot a glance at Rico. "What's up with her? I mean, she's usually cheerful, but this is over-the-top weird."

"I heard that," Laurel called out. "I can live with weird. Beats boring, don't you think, Rico?"

Carissa's frown deepened. "Did you get into some wacky weed last night? Are you high?"

Laurel laughed, carrying another loaded vase past Carissa and Rico. "I'm not high, and I'm not wearing any underwear under this dress."

"Okay, boss, you just crossed from weird to creepy." With her free hand, she poked a finger in her ear. "I didn't need to know that you're trotting around all these innocent flowers, al fresco. Great, now I can't unsee—no, unhear—your undergarment revelation."

Laurel laughed and waved at her assistant. "Go drink your coffee, Carissa."

Carissa trudged toward the door. "I'm afraid no amount of coffee will make it better." Her look, demeanor and the way she spoke reminded Laurel of Eeyore from the Winnie the Pooh franchise.

Laurel grinned, enjoying throwing off her assistant and her one-night-stand lover. Why not have fun while winning the heart of the man who'd vowed to walk away?

After they'd completed loading the van with the day's orders, the memorial bouquet and the framed photograph of Chris, they set off on their morning deliveries.

This was one of her favorite parts of owning a flower shop. She loved to see the smiles on the faces of her customers when they received a floral gift from a loved one.

They traveled from house to house, some out on winding mountain roads a couple of miles from town. Laurel had thought she'd known her way around her community growing up there, but delivering flowers constantly showed her there were a lot of roads she'd never even known existed. Some were buried in deep forests. Others climbed the sides of mountains, with amazing views that made Laurel proud to live in Colorado.

Near noon, they came to their final delivery stop —the Divine Chapel in the heart of Fool's Gold.

Having smiled, laughed and spread cheer all morning, Laurel's mood turned somber. Today, they'd say goodbye to a friend.

Laurel led the way into the church and stopped at the secretary's office to let her know they were there and to find out where to place the floral arrangement.

"Mrs. Monahan wanted a small table set up in the front of the chapel. I've been answering phone calls about our yard sale this weekend, coordinating food trucks, portable toilets and security and haven't had time to get the table out of the storage closet." As if on cue, her phone rang.

"We can take care of it," Rico said. "Just point the way."

"The storage room is in the Sunday school wing. The key should be in the door. I was moving supplies in earlier. The tablecloth is on a shelf above the table." She lifted the phone off the cradle. "Divine Chapel, this is Melanie."

Laurel led the way out of the secretary's office, down a short hallway, turned right and took a left at a T-intersection. "This is the Sunday school wing," she said.

Only one door had a key in the lock. "This must be it." Laurel turned the key and opened the door to a small storage room with shelves lining the wall filled with toilet paper, cleaning liquids, cleaning rags, mops, a vacuum and more. In a tight corner stood a small pedestal table.

Laurel flipped the light switch and stepped into the small closet.

"Let me," Rico said, following her in.

The closet was barely big enough for the items stored there. Two grown adults filled what little space was left. The single light bulb overhead flickered, blinked out and came back on.

Laurel felt the walls closing in around her. "I'll just wait in the hall."

She tried to step around Rico, but the mop bucket was in the way on one side and the vacuum on the other.

Her heartbeat kicked into high gear.

If she didn't get out soon, she'd go from okay to full-on-panic.

"Sorry. I didn't mean to crowd you." Rico backed out of the closet and moved aside so Laurel could quickly and easily exit.

She grabbed a tablecloth off the shelf above the

table and practically dove through the door. Once in the hallway, she slowed, smoothed her hands down her dress and forced air in and out of her lungs.

Rico's gaze followed her every movement. He didn't comment but waited until she was in full control before he stepped back into the closet to retrieve the table.

When he came out, she closed the door and led the way down a maze of hallways to the double doors leading into the chapel.

Light streamed through colorful stained-glass windows, making pretty patterns across the floors and pews.

Rico carried the table to the front of the rows of pews and placed it in the center of the space. An organ stood on a dais to the right and a raised podium to the left.

"I'll drape the table while you fetch the arrangement," Laurel said.

When Rico hesitated, Laurel's lips twisted. "We're in an empty church. I'll be fine for the few short minutes you take to get the flowers." She gave him a pointed look. "Go."

Reluctantly, Rico left.

Laurel spread the gold cloth over the table and made sure it fell evenly over the sides to the floor.

A noise echoed in the chapel, making her glance up and look around.

Since it had been an echo, she couldn't pinpoint

its origin and assumed it was the old building settling.

Rico appeared, carrying the crystal vase of white lilies and roses.

As he neared the table, Laurel held out her hands. "Here, I'll take that."

When he passed the vase to her, his hands connected with hers, and he jerked back.

Laurel didn't have her hands firmly around the heavy vase when Rico let go. As it slipped through her fingers, she bent quickly, catching it before it crashed to the floor. The water in the vase sloshed over the rim onto the floor, but the arrangement remained intact, if a little wonky.

"Whew!" Laurel breathed. "That was close."

"Sorry," Rico said. "I thought you had it."

"I do now." She smiled now that disaster had been averted and then frowned.

"What's wrong?" Rico asked.

"I forgot the framed photo. Can you get it while I fix the flowers?"

Rico spun and hurried out of the chapel.

Laurel quickly rearranged the misaligned flowers and stood back to inspect the table and the vase. That's when she noticed the puddle of water on the floor.

She left the chapel and headed for the storage room where she'd seen mops and cleaning cloths. All she needed was a cloth. The spill wasn't enough to warrant a mop.

Thankfully, the key was still in the door handle.

Laurel turned the key and opened the door. Reaching inside, she flipped the light switch. The bulb blinked on and then flickered.

She didn't have time to worry about it. She left the door open wide to shed enough light for her to see the cleaning rags on the shelf. She stepped inside. As she reached for a cloth, the door swung closed behind her.

With the cloth in hand, she turned, wrapped her hand around the doorknob and tried to turn it.

It didn't move.

The light overhead flickered and went out, plunging Laurel into pitch darkness and back into that hole in the ground at the side of a mountain in Syria.

CHAPTER 12

RICO HURRIED out to the van for the framed photograph only to find the back window on the van had been tagged with the same symbol used on Laurel's car. A big, black U had been drawn on the window with a black dot in the middle.

Despite the bad feeling pressing down on Rico's chest, he yanked open the back door and reached for the framed photo of Chris Monahan. It lay face up, not leaning against the sidewall of the van like they'd left it. A perfect black rose lay across the glass.

Rico snatched both the frame and the rose and ran back into the church. His heart raced, and his gut clenched. When he reached the chapel, all the air left his lungs.

The neatly arranged flowers stood on the pedestal table, front and center.

Laurel was gone.

"Laurel!" he called out, his voice echoing off the high ceilings.

She couldn't have gone far. He hadn't been gone more than two minutes, if that. Running up the center aisle, he checked both rows of pews in case she'd tripped and fallen amongst them. Though, there was no reason for her to step between the pews when she was there only to deliver the memorial flowers.

"Laurel!" he yelled as he checked in the area behind the podium where the choir likely sat on the row of benches.

Not there.

Rico turned and ran for the secretary's office. Her door was closed with a sign hanging on the outside.

GONE TO LUNCH,

Frantic by now, he ran down the hallways, calling her name. "Laurel!"

When he reached the Sunday school wing, a sound caught his attention. Someone was knocking.

"Laurel?" Rico tried door after door. Each one was locked.

Wasn't this the hallway with the supply room? They'd spotted it easily when they'd come for the pedestal table. It had a key in the doorknob.

Rico looked at all the doorknobs. None of them had a key in them.

The knocking started again.

"Laurel?"

"Rico?" her muffled voice came from a door halfway down the hallway on the left.

Rico reached it in three giant strides, gripped the handle and tried to twist it. The door was locked.

"Rico?" Laurel's voice sounded through the door panel. "I can't get out. The door's locked, and the light burned out."

"Don't worry, I'll get you out." He had no idea how he'd get her out without the key. The secretary was gone for lunch.

"Stay put," he said. "I'll be right back.'

She laughed. The sound was shaky at best. "I've got nowhere else to go. Hurry,"

Rico sprang into action, racing through the halls. He checked the secretary's office.

She wasn't back. Most likely, she had a key somewhere in there, but he didn't have time to wait. Laurel was in a dark, tight place. It was only a matter of time before she panicked—if she hadn't already.

The only other choice he had was the crowbar he'd spotted in the back of the van.

Back out to the van, he slung open the rear door, crawled in and snagged the crowbar from where it hung in clips on the sidewall.

In just a few seconds, he was back in the church, standing in front of the locked supply room.

"Laurel?"

"I'm still here," she answered.

He chuckled. "Good. I'd hate to think I was about

to damage church property for no reason. Stand back."

She huffed. "Funny. There's only enough space to stand. There is no additional room for backing away."

"Then at least close your eyes."

"Done," she said. "What are you going to do?"

"Pry the door open and get you the hell out."

"I like the sound of that," she said softly.

"Hanging in there?" he asked as he fit the flat edge of the crowbar between the door and the doorframe, just above the doorknob.

After three attempts to dislodge the door from the frame, using his arms and back, Rico threw all his anger and frustration into a sidekick that hit the crowbar hard enough the door lock splintered, and the door popped open.

Laurel launched herself at him, wrapping her arms around his neck and her legs around his waist.

Rico dropped the crowbar and crushed Laurel to his chest, burying his face in her hair. "When I came into that chapel, and you were gone..." His voice faded off. He leaned her back against the hall wall and stared down into her eyes. "Are you okay? Having a panic attack?"

"I'm okay," she said. "I focused on breathing in and out. Then you came, and now, I'm okay." She smiled up at him.

"Did you bring the key with you into the store-room?" Rico asked.

Laurel shook her head. "No. It's in the door. It's just that the door swung closed behind me."

Rico frowned. "The key wasn't in the door."

"Yes, it is." She turned to look at the empty door-knob. "Well, it was."

His arms tightened around her back. "I think your secret tormentor was here."

Her eyes widened. "How can you be sure?"

"The secretary is out to lunch. No one else is supposed to be in the church, and someone left a gift of a black rose in the van on top of Chris Monahan's photo."

The color drained from Laurel's ace. "A black rose?"

He nodded. "Come on, I want to search the church to see if our prankster is still here. You'll have to come with me because I'm not letting you out of my sight."

Her smile warmed him. "I'll happily tag along if it means I get to be with you and not locked in a dark closet." Laurel held up the rag she'd come to retrieve. "Could we go by way of the chapel first?" She laughed, albeit shakily. "I need to clean up a spill."

After Laurel cleaned up the spill, Rico led the way on his search.

"Just stay behind me," he said. "We don't know if he's armed."

Laurel followed Rico through the church, never more than a foot or two behind him, at times with her hand on his back. "Do you think he might escalate to physical attacks?"

"I don't know," he said. "It's best to be prepared."

Since most of the rooms were empty or locked, the search didn't take long. They emerged through the back entrance where Rico had parked the van.

Rico held the passenger door for Laurel. "Let's get out of here."

"You don't have to ask me twice." Laurel shivered as she secured her seatbelt. "I wouldn't come back if not for the memorial."

When Rico passed Laurel's Florals, Laurel looked back at her building.

She glanced across at Rico. "Where are we going?"

"Sheriff's office," Rico said.

"Why?"

"He needs to know about the latest threat."

"A black rose?" Laurel cocked an eyebrow.

"It wasn't just the rose," he said, pulling into the parking lot in front of the sheriff's office. He shifted into park and met her gaze. "You didn't lock yourself in that supply closet, or paint the Christian symbol on your car window."

"I could've been mistaken about the key being in the lock," Laurel said. "The door could've swung closed on its own. It just doesn't seem that dangerous or worthy of bothering the sheriff."

Rico held firm. "Better to have too much information than not enough. Things start adding up. Dots can be connected. When we're done in town, I want to head out to Lost Valley Ranch and see if Jake and his computer guys have surfaced anything else of use."

"I still have a business to run," Laurel pointed out.

"While I'm talking to the sheriff, you can call Carissa and check in. If she's swamped, we'll go to the shop." He opened his door and dropped down from the van.

Laurel met him at the front of the vehicle. "I just feel like this is a bit trivial compared to real crimes. What do we have so far? A flag, slashed tires, a Christian symbol and a black rose. No one has actually threatened me with bodily harm."

"Being locked in a supply closet," Rico added.

"I wasn't hurt," Laurel pointed out.

"Maybe not, but someone is targeting you. We don't want to wait for him to hurt you to alert the authorities. Especially if he's connected with ISIS, it might only be a matter of time. At the very least, you have a stalker. That's creepy all by itself."

Laurel's lips twisted. "It is. And you're right." She hooked her hand through his elbow. "Lead the way."

He glanced down at her, his eyes narrowed.

"What?" she looked up at him innocently.

"You gave up arguing too quickly."

"I'm a big believer in the statement that life's too

short to sweat the small stuff." She pulled her cell phone out of her pocket as they entered the sheriff's office. "I'll stand in the corner by the window and call Carissa while you report to the sheriff." She smiled and walked over to the window, placing the call.

Other than the scare of her being locked in the supply closet, Laurel had been more agreeable since he'd told her he was going to have Jake replace him with someone else to provide Laurel's protection. She'd smiled all morning at her customers and him as though trading him for a different protector was exactly what she needed.

It rubbed on Rico's nerves. After making love with her the night before and her begging him not to ask Jake for a substitute, she'd made a complete recovery and turnaround.

Rico knew he shouldn't let it bother him.

But it did.

When he'd walked into the chapel and discovered she was gone, he'd nearly had a coronary. His mind had gone through all the worst scenarios. Finding her locked in the closet both relieved him and punched him in the gut. Her stalker had to be familiar enough with Laurel to know locking her in a tight place would trigger her PTSD-induced panic attacks. It harmed her mentally, if not physically.

Rico wasn't the right man to love Laurel. He might not be the right one to protect her, given he had made the mistake of falling for her, but the thought of walking away from her and trusting someone else with her safety tore at Rico.

He wasn't sure he could do it. He couldn't abandon her when she was in danger. The only other choice was to see this job through. Once she was safe, he'd step out of her life.

Sheriff Faulkner emerged from his office and shook Rico's hand. After Rico explained the latest events, the sheriff thanked him for the information and assured him they'd look into it. He'd let them know if they found evidence pointing to Laurel's stalker.

Laurel joined him and smiled up at the sheriff. "Sheriff Faulkner."

"Miss Layne, it appears as though you have a stalker."

"Lucky me," she said with a crooked smile.

"I'm glad you two stopped in. We lifted several sets of fingerprints off the package with the flag. I need both of your prints to rule you out."

Laurel and Rico filled out fingerprint cards, thanked the sheriff for his patience and left.

Back in the van, Rico looked at Laurel. "Well? Is Carissa swamped, and you need to jump in and save the day?"

Laurel's lips twisted. "Not exactly. She said it's been slow, and she's all caught up. She's spent the past hour cleaning and dusting."

"We're going out to the ranch." He shifted into reverse.

"Actually, that works well for me. I can touch bases with RJ to finalize the location to scatter Chris's ashes in the mountains and see if there will be enough four-wheelers and side-by-sides to transport everyone who wants to come." She paused. "However, I'd like to leave the van at the shop. Do you mind if we take your truck?"

"My pleasure," Rico said. "Have you checked on your car?"

"I called the tire place after I called Carissa. They had to order the tires. They'll be in tomorrow, and they'll put them on right away. I should be able to pick up my car tomorrow afternoon."

Rico parked the van behind the shop and walked into the flower shop with Laurel.

Laurel's assistant was with a customer.

While they waited for Carissa to complete the sale, Laurel wandered around the shop, rearranging flowers in the buckets, even though they looked fine to Rico. Finally, she stopped beside Rico and sighed. "She's good."

He chuckled. "That's a good thing, right?"

Laurel nodded. "I got lucky when she applied here."

Carissa walked the customer to the door, thanked her for the business and then turned with a smile, tilting her head to one side. "You know...you two make a cute couple."

Rico frowned. "We're not—"

"You think so?" Laurel cut in. "I don't know... I usually gravitate to taller men."

Carissa shook her head. "You're so petite, a taller man would make you look like a child. Rico's a perfect height for you." She smiled at Rico. "How tall are you?"

His frown deepening, Rico replied automatically. "Five-eleven."

"Hmm," Carissa's brow wrinkled. "You might be borderline tall for Laurel." Her smile returned. "I stand by my original observation. You two make a cute couple."

Rico had nothing to say. They weren't a couple and never would be. "Ready to go?"

Laurel grinned. "As long as Carissa doesn't need me."

"I can hold down the fort. Go." She shooed them toward the back door. "Hopefully, you're going somewhere fun."

"Lost Valley Ranch," Laurel informed her. "We'll be back in town for the memorial and then go back out to the ranch afterward to scatter ashes."

Carissa's smile faded. "I'm sorry about your friend. It must have been really hard on his wife."

Laurel nodded. "They were newlyweds when we

deployed to Syria. He wasn't the same person when he returned."

"Must be hard being separated from your loved ones for so long." Carissa clapped her hands together, and her smile returned. "Today's another day. The sun is shining, and it's good to be alive. Enjoy the drive out to the ranch. I'll take care of things here and lock up at closing."

Laurel followed Rico to his truck.

He opened the door and offered a hand to help her in.

Before making love, she'd been adamant about being independent.

Laurel smiled up at him and took his hand. "You are the perfect height." She murmured something beneath her breath that sounded suspiciously like *for kissing.*

When her hand touched his, the electricity that zapped through him almost made him pull away. To do so at that moment would have caused her a misstep, and she might have fallen off the running boards.

Of course., he'd be there to catch her. She'd end up in his arms, and her lips would be so close…

If he wasn't mistaken, she'd said he was the perfect height for kissing. He'd prove it.

And what would that really prove, besides the fact he was falling for this woman?

Where would that lead?

Nowhere.

He couldn't be with her until he could control his nightmares and the resulting violence they inspired.

Damn, but he wanted to hold her, kiss her and make love to her all over again. One night with Laurel wasn't nearly enough.

But it had to be.

Rico backed out of his parking space and drove away from the flower shop, heading for the Lost Valley Ranch. He'd get with Jake and maybe bring up a video conference with Hank and his computer guy, Swede. They had to come up with some potential suspects.

So far, they had no idea who was tormenting Laurel by tapping into every trigger that could send her spiraling into a mental breakdown.

Yet, she remained upbeat and strong.

Rico's heart swelled.

After all Laurel had been through, she chose to be strong, independent and happy.

Thus far, the threats hadn't materialized as specific physical dangers to Laurel. Rico couldn't let up on his vigilance to keep her safe—and he couldn't let someone else take over the responsibility.

When they arrived at Lost Valley Ranch, RJ Tate was walking up from the barn, brushing dust from her jeans.

Rico parked, dropped down from the truck and rounded the front to open Laurel's door for her.

RJ met them at the steps to the front porch. "Here to see Jake?"

Rico nodded. "We are."

"I also wanted to make sure we're a go for spreading Chris Monahan's ashes this afternoon after the memorial," Laurel said. "Is there a particular location you recommend?"

RJ glanced over her shoulder at the ridge behind her. "Mrs. Monahan came by yesterday afternoon. I took her up the trail past the old mine to the bluffs beyond. The view is spectacular, and the breeze will be nice to carry his ashes away."

"Do you have enough all-terrain vehicles to get maybe a dozen people up there?"

RJ nodded. "We have two side-by-sides that will carry four people each and several four-wheelers. I'll have them ready and staged for when your party arrives."

"Thank you," Laurel said. "Let me know what we owe you."

RJ held up her hands. "Not a thing. You're family."

RJ's generosity warmed Rico's heart. Having been in Fool's Gold for only a few days, he couldn't get over how connected people were in the community. It made him glad he'd chosen to come to work for Brotherhood Protectors. He'd found another team with the expanded reach of a community.

RJ started up the steps to the porch. "Monahan's death was tragic. We lose too many of our veterans to suicide. His wife said he was going to therapy, but it wasn't enough. He'd suffered so much in Syria and then came home to more tragedy when his wife miscarried."

Laurel followed RJ. "It was more than he could take."

"I don't know how his wife is holding up," RJ said. "Gunny and I talked. We'd like to host dinner this evening for your people after the memorial and distribution of his ashes. It won't be fancy. We'll grill out and let everyone hang out on the porch. Kind of like a wake or celebration of life. I imagine most folks will leave tomorrow."

Laurel hugged RJ. "Thank you. That would be lovely."

RJ turned to Rico, where he stood at the bottom of the steps. "Jake should be in the war room."

Rico climbed the steps. "What you're doing for Mrs. Monahan is very generous."

"It's the least we can do for our men and women in uniform, like you and Laurel, who've given so much for our country." She held the door open for them. "Now, I'm going to clean up. I have KP duty in preparation for this afternoon. Gunny won't let me into the kitchen smelling like horse manure." She left them in the great room and climbed the stairs to the second floor.

Rico led the way through the dining room and into the kitchen.

"Rico. Laurel," Gunny greeted them with a nod, his hands pressing deeply into a mound of dough he was kneading. "I'd shake your hands, but I'm up to my elbows in dinner rolls." He winked and tipped his head toward the basement door. "Jake's in the war room."

As they passed the old Marine, Laurel leaned up on her toes and pressed a kiss to his grizzled cheek. "Thanks for everything, Gunny. You're a good human."

The old Marine's cheeks turned a ruddy red. "Get on out of here."

Laurel laughed. "You're not fooling me, Gunny. Beneath that gruff exterior is an old softy." She kissed his cheek again. "Don't you change."

Rico's heart pinched hard in his chest. He loved that Laurel had people in her life like RJ and Gunny looking out for her. She'd be okay if he moved on. The thought made him glad for her and sad for himself.

Damn his nightmares!

The therapist said they had to do with survivor's guilt over the death of his battle buddy, Bert. He blamed himself for his friend's death because he hadn't been able to save him.

Until he forgave himself for failing to have his friend's six, he'd continue to fight the same battle and lose in his dreams.

Laurel led the way down the stairs into the basement war room, the epicenter of the Brotherhood Protectors Colorado division.

Jake sat at the huge conference table, his attention on a large screen at the opposite end. An image of a man with white-blond hair filled the screen, larger than life,

Jake turned and grinned at Laurel and Rico. "Oh, good. Just in time." He stood, hugged Laurel and shook Rico's hand. "You remember Axel Svenson?"

Rico nodded. "I do. We crossed paths on a mission to Somalia when I was fresh out of BUD/S training. Saved my ass if I recall." He nodded at the big Viking. "Hey, Swede."

"Rico," Swede dipped his head in greeting. "Welcome to Brotherhood Protectors. You landed with a good guy. Cog's a good man."

"I wouldn't be here if he wasn't," Rico said. "I understand you're our go-to guy for technology and data mining. Any news on our situation here?"

"We were just discussing it," Jake, aka Cog, said.

"The Department of Homeland Security arrested a dozen ISIS wannabes who'd been stockpiling weapons in the hills."

Rico grinned. "That's good news. That means Laurel's troubles are over."

A relieved smile curled Laurel's lips. "That would be great."

Jake and Swede both shook their heads.

"Sorry," Swede said. "They arrested them *yesterday* morning."

Laurel's brow twisted. "Yesterday morning? I don't understand. I received the flag just before noon yesterday, and my tires were slashed last night. And what about today when someone locked me in the supply closet at the church? Did they miss someone in their arrest?"

Swede shook his head. "The men they arrested were closer to Vail. None of them had been anywhere near Fool's Gold."

"Is there another branch of their organization here?" Rico asked.

Swede shook his head. "Before their arrest, DHS would only say they were in the Colorado Rockies. Now that they're in custody, they've released more information. They weren't the guy or guys stalking Miss Layne."

Laurel sighed. "So, we're back to the drawing board?"

"That about sums it up," Jake said. "Since your troubles didn't begin until Chris Monahan committed suicide and requested his memorial be conducted in Fool's Gold, we're running background checks on the people coming to pay their respects."

Laurel frowned. "You think someone from our old unit might be stalking me?"

"Did you have a run-in with any of the guys prior to leaving your unit?" Swede asked.

She shook her head. "No. I got along fine with all the medics, laboratory technicians, Chris, Colonel Estep and our administrative staff."

"Did anyone come on to you?" Jake asked.

Laurel continued to shake her head. "No. Any fraternizing is forbidden while deployed. I wouldn't have risked my commission."

"Did anyone show an inordinate amount of interest in you or follow you around more than necessary?" Swede persisted.

"If someone did, I didn't notice. I played by the rules. I was there to do my job." Laurel's gaze bounced to the corners the room as if she were looking to the past, trying to remember.

"Did Dr. Estep ever show more than a professional interest in you?" Jake asked.

An image of the doctor flashed into Rico's mind. The man had been sitting too close to Laurel the night before at their reunion and had draped his arm across the back of her chair.

"Colonel Estep never once made any unprofessional advances against me," Laurel said. "Why would you think such a thing?"

"In his wife's request for divorce, she listed violence and infidelity."

"He had an affair?" Laurel's eyebrows met over her nose. "I can't picture it. The man was always professional around his staff. Back at our duty station in San Antonio, he wouldn't even go out for drinks with us."

"Estep left the Watering Hole before anyone else," Rico pointed out.

Laurel stared at the conference table. "That doesn't mean he slashed my tires."

"He came to your shop yesterday," Rico said. "None of the other men who are here for the memorial have stopped in."

"We're not saying Dr. Estep is your stalker," Jake said. "We're just saying he's someone to keep an eye on."

"Any of the men here for the memorial, for that matter," Swede added.

"What motivation could they have for stalking me and scaring me with the ISIS bullshit?" Laurel asked.

"That's where we're stumped," Jake admitted. "Everyone in Fool's Gold loves you. Admittedly, we're grasping at straws."

"Maybe PTSD has gotten the better of the doctor like it did Chris Monahan. Maybe he can't stand to see you getting on with your life when his is falling apart," Swede suggested.

"Maybe he wants to bring you down to his level of misery?" Jake shrugged. "Just keep your eyes open. PTSD can do shitty things to good people."

Rico couldn't stand the distress etched on Laurel's face. He slid an arm around her waist. "If her stalker is one of the people here for the reunion, hopefully, they'll be leaving soon. We'll remain vigilant until they do and the incidents cease."

Laurel nodded. "What this is doing is making me paranoid." She squared her shoulders. "I'm ready to get this memorial over with."

Rico couldn't agree more.

He hoped Laurel's troubles went away with the people who'd come to pay tribute to a fallen comrade. However, he didn't like the idea that Laurel's stalker would get away without retribution for scaring her.

She leaned into him.

Rico might not be the right partner for Laurel, but he was going to keep her close until the troubles were resolved. They just had to get through the memorial at the chapel, spreading the ashes in the hills and a wake surrounded by Jake, Gunny and other members of the Brotherhood Protectors. Between all of them, they should be able to keep one florist safe.

CHAPTER 13

LAUREL SAT beside Rico in the front pew of the chapel as mournful organ music echoed off the high ceilings.

The members of her old unit trickled in, taking seats behind Laurel, some talking quietly amongst themselves.

When the music stopped, Dr. Estep escorted Mandy Monahan up the aisle to take a seat on the opposite side of the aisle from Laurel and Rico.

The doctor sat beside her.

Reverend Nelson, the church pastor, came out of a side door and stood at the podium.

"Thank you for coming to Fool's Gold to celebrate the life of Christian Monahan, husband, son, friend and brother in arms." The reverend went on to quote scripture and gave a brief biography of Chris

Monahan. When he finished, he nodded to Mandy Monahan.

She approached the podium, dabbing at red-rimmed eyes with a tissue. After a long pause, she looked at the people in the pews and gave a weak smile. "Chris would be happy to know he wasn't forgotten. He was a kind man with a big heart. He'd do anything for anyone, especially his country and military comrades."

Tears slipped down her cheeks. "When he got orders to deploy, we moved our wedding date up so that we could get married before he left instead of waiting until he returned. We had a short but magical honeymoon on the Riverwalk in San Antonio. A couple of weeks later, he shipped out with his unit." She dabbed at her cheeks. "That was the last time I saw the man I married."

Laurel's heart pinched tightly in her chest, remembering how happy Chris had been and how everyone had teased him about his honeymoon and asked when the baby was due.

"I found out I was pregnant two months into his deployment. On our next video call, I told him." Mandy smiled through her tears. "He was so happy. He couldn't wait to find out the sex of our child and to come home to be with me when I gave birth." She looked to the corner of the church, blinking back fresh tears.

Tears slipped from Laurel's eyes. She knew what

was coming in this story Mandy was telling. She'd lived it.

Rico reached out to take her hand and held it in his lap.

"When men in uniform arrived at my door, I couldn't believe what they were telling me. My husband of a couple of months had been captured?" She shook her head, her face pale. "The commander's wife stayed with me that night. Other wives took turns staying with me over the next couple of weeks. I was a mess. I couldn't eat, couldn't sleep, couldn't imagine what was happening to Chris. I was so upset I started hemorrhaging. The wife of the day called an ambulance. I was rushed to the hospital. My obstetrician informed me that because of the stress I'd been under, my body spontaneously aborted our baby." Her voice caught on a sob. "They released me the next day. I went back to my apartment and told the wife who'd been tagged to stay with me that day to go home. People brought me food. The commander himself came over to conduct a wellness check. I told them all I was fine."

Laurel knew better.

"Then the commander came a couple of days later to accompany me to Bethesda, Maryland. They'd rescued Chris and were bringing him there for treatment before sending him home. I was happy he was coming home and terrified at the same time. How could I tell him I'd let myself get so worked up that I'd lost our baby."

Mandy stopped talking and stared at her hands resting on the podium. "I loved the man I married. I thought he and I could get through everything together." She looked up. "But he wasn't the man I'd married anymore. They'd beaten and tortured that man out of him. He said the only thing that kept him from giving up was knowing he had a wife and child to come home to."

Mandy's head bowed. "He only had me. The doctors told him what they'd done to him had rendered him sterile. He'd never have children of his own. I told him I didn't care as long as I had him. He didn't believe me. It all went downhill from there. And you know how this story ended."

Mandy looked up, her gaze going to Laurel and Dr. Estep. "At least he isn't suffering anymore. Thank you for coming, and thank you for being the good part of my husband's life." She left the podium and sat next to Dr. Estep.

Reverend Nelson appeared. "If anyone would like to say something, you're welcome to do so at this time."

Dr. Estep stood and turned to face Mandy and the others. "Chris was a highly skilled professional in the operating room, but I'll never forget his bravery in the face of captivity. No human should have to endure what he did." He held Laurel's gaze for a long moment and then took his seat.

Dark images flooded her memory. Those suppressed images of the three of them in the torture room, forced to witness each other's pain, their captors demanding their secrets. Secrets they didn't have.

Laurel's chest tightened to the point she couldn't breathe.

Rico's fingers tightened around hers, squeezing gently. "Breathe," he whispered against her ear.

At the sound of Rico's warm, comforting tone, Laurel forced air into her lungs and let it out slowly.

One of the medics stood and told an anecdote of a frightened patient Chris had calmed by telling him really bad jokes. By the time he'd knocked him out for the operation, everyone in the room had been laughing.

Laurel was last to stand. "I could choose to remember Chris when they pulled us out of that ISIS compound, dirty, scarred, beaten and a shadow of the man who'd gone in, but that wouldn't do the man justice. He was a good friend, a loving husband and a consummate professional." She turned toward the photograph of Chris before he'd deployed. "I choose to remember his smile and how he'd sing 'I feel good' and play the air guitar when he walked into the hospital, whether it was at our home station or in the field. We lost a good one. He's gone but not forgotten."

The reverend closed the service with a prayer.

Laurel stood. "For those who want to be there when we release Chris's ashes, we'll meet out at the Lost Valley Ranch in twenty minutes. Gunny and RJ have ATVs waiting for us to take Chris to one of the most scenic points on the ranch for our final goodbye. Rico and I will lead the way if you want to caravan out there. There will be a meal provided afterward for those who choose to stay."

They filed out of the church and into their respective vehicles. Mandy climbed into the Mercedes sports car with Dr. Estep; the others shared rides and lined up behind Rico's truck.

Twenty minutes later, they arrived at the ranch, parked their vehicles and gathered around the ATVs RJ and Gunny had positioned outside the barn.

RJ was there to greet them with the ranch mechanic, JoJo Ramirez, and her fiancé, Max Thornton.

Laurel smiled every time she saw this couple. They were perfect together. Petite, badass JoJo had met her match in Max, and they couldn't be happier.

RJ waved a hand at the pair. "JoJo and Max will lead you up the trail. I'd go, but Gunny and I are manning the oven and the grill. We'll have hot food and cold beer waiting for you when you get back. A word of warning. The sun sets earlier in the valleys.

Don't wait until dusk to descend. JoJo and Max will let you know when it's time to head back." She stepped back. "See you in a little while."

JoJo and Max slid into a two-seater ATV with a small utility truck bed on the back filled with an assortment of equipment—an ice chest, a roll of barbed wire, rope and a first aid kit.

Laurel glanced up at Rico. "Do you mind if I drive?"

He waved a hand toward the vehicle. "Knock yourself out."

Laurel slipped into the driver's seat of the second utility vehicle, a four-seater. Rico sat beside her. Dr. Estep, carrying the urn with Chris's ashes, and Mandy claimed the back seat.

The other men chose individual four-wheelers.

When all vehicles were started, JoJo and Max led them through a gate RJ opened, across a pasture and up a hill. The trail wound around the sides of hills and through the trees, climbing higher.

They passed what appeared to be an old mine. Laurel pointed to the entrance. "These hills are full of old mine shafts. People are warned to stay out, that they're dangerous, but they still go in, thinking it's cool to explore. Most entrances have been boarded up to keep trespassers out." Laurel frowned. "This one was boarded up not long ago. Remind me to ask JoJo why it's open now."

Several minutes later, they arrived at the top of a

ridge Laurel had visited several times during the daylight. One time, late one summer, she'd gone out in the evening with RJ and Gunny. They'd spread blankets and lay on the ground, waiting for it to get dark to watch a meteor shower.

It was a perfect location for their final goodbye to Chris.

JoJo and Max parked their ATV below the ridgeline and turned off the engine.

Laurel parked beside them, shut down the engine and got out. The others pulled in and shut down their engines.

Dr. Estep climbed out with the urn. Rico helped Mandy out.

They all walked to the edge of the ridge.

"Don't stand too close," JoJo warned. "It's a one-hundred-foot drop nearly straight down."

Dr. Estep held the urn while Rico unscrewed the top and pulled out the plastic bag containing Chris Monahan's ashes. He handed it to Mandy.

She stood near the edge with her husband's ashes. Everyone formed a line upwind of Mandy.

"I miss you, my love," she said. "When you see our baby, tell her that her mama loves her."

She opened the bag and poured a little out at a time.

The wind picked up the ashes and carried them, swirling in a beautiful stream of gray.

Rico rested his hand on the small of Laurel's back.

She leaned into him. "He's in a better place now. When I die, I don't want to be buried in the ground." She shivered. "Bring me here. This is where I want my ashes released so I can fly on the wind." As if on cue, the breeze lifted strands of her hair, swirling it around her face.

Rico brushed a strand behind her ear and bent to press his lips to her forehead. "Do me a favor, and don't die anytime soon."

She smiled up at him. "Would you miss me?"

He nodded.

Her heart soared. The man clearly liked her. If they could work through his dreams, they might eventually have a future together.

Mandy struggled a little with the plastic bag.

Dr. Estep stepped forward to help.

While they worked to release all the ashes, Laurel turned to JoJo. "I noticed the old mine entrance we passed wasn't boarded up like it was. What's up with that?"

JoJo's lips pressed together. "A mining company approached Gunny about reevaluating some of the old mines around here. They sent a geologist down to determine if that mine might be a candidate for some newfangled mining techniques. They were out here earlier today and will be back again tomorrow, so they left it open. None of the lodge guests should be this far up the mountain while they're working there."

"Hey, JoJo." One of the medics got JoJo's attention and pointed to the tallest peak visible from where they stood. "What mountain is that?" he asked.

JoJo lifted her chin toward it. "That's Pike's Peak. If you're not leaving soon, you should go up there. They have a nice visitor's center and an incredible view."

"Have you been up to the top of Pike's Peak?" Laurel asked Rico.

He glanced at the mountain and shook his head. "I haven't."

"If you'd like, I'll take you up this weekend."

"I'd like that," he said.

A scream ripped through the air.

Laurel spun to find Mandy lying on the ground, her legs dangling over the edge of the ridge. "Help me!" she cried.

Everyone rushed forward.

Rico reached her first and pulled her away from the edge onto her feet.

"What happened," Laurel asked.

Tears spilled down Mandy's cheeks. "It's Dr. Estep." She choked on a sob. "He...he tried to push me over the edge."

Laurel looked around. "Mandy, where is Dr. Estep?"

Mandy sobbed and pointed to the edge. "He tried to push me over the edge... I did the only thing I could do. I dropped to the ground. He was pushing so hard that when I went down, he tripped over me and fell."

JoJo, Max and Rico leaned over the edge.

"He's caught on a ledge about fifty feet down," Rico said.

"He's not moving," JoJo noted.

When Laurel moved forward, Rico's arm shot out. "Stay back. There's loose gravel on the edge.

"There's a rope in my ATV," JoJo said. "It might be long enough to reach him."

One of the medics pulled his cell phone from his pocket, stared at the screen and shook his head. "No service. I can go down to the lodge and call 911."

JoJo shook her head. "Stay here. The last thing we need is people taking the wrong turn and running off another cliff. I'll take one of the four-wheelers down. I know the way and can get there faster." She ran for the closest four-wheeler, hopped on, started the engine and disappeared down the trail.

Mandy stood back from the edge, her body shaking with the force of her sobs.

While the men rushed to secure the rope to a tree, Laurel wrapped her arms around Mandy. "It's okay. You're going to be okay."

"He tried...to kill...me," she said between sobs.

"But he didn't," Laurel smoothed a hand over Mandy's back. "You're safe. We won't let anything happen to you."

"Oh, Laurel, it wasn't supposed to be like this."

"Chris is free now," Laurel said. "You're going to be all right. Just give yourself time."

"No. He was supposed to do his deployment and come back the same Chris I married. We were supposed to have a baby and be a family by now. I wasn't supposed to be a widow at twenty-seven."

"Oh, Mandy," Laurel's hurt for the young widow. "Things don't always turn out the way we planned. You have to cherish your good memories and keep looking forward."

"Like you?" Mandy shook her head. "I'm not as strong. Chris wasn't as strong."

"I'm not that strong. I make the choice every day to be happy. If I'm sad, I fake it until I feel it."

"It's just not fair," Mandy whispered, more tears slipping down her cheeks.

Laurel glanced over Mandy's shoulder as the men dropped the rope over the edge.

"I'm going down," Max said.

"No," Rico said. "I'm shorter and weigh less than any of you. Pulling me up will be easier for you."

"But I'm a medic," one of the guys said.

"Are you trained to rappel?" Rico asked.

The man shook his head. "No."

"Now's not the time to teach you," Rico said. "I have enough first aid training to get his breathing or heart going again." Rico checked the seat he'd fashioned out of rope and slipped the long rope around the carabiner. Holding the downward length behind him, he backed over the ledge.

His gaze met Laurel's for a moment, then he disappeared below the ridge.

Laurel's breath caught in her throat as she held Mandy away from the edge, wishing she could watch Rico as he descended to where Dr. Estep had landed.

No one spoke for several long seconds.

Then Max said, "He's down."

Silence reined for several more seconds until Rico's voice called out, "He's alive!"

"Oh, thank God," Laurel murmured.

Mandy stiffened, and she leaned away from Laurel, her eyes wide. "You have to take me down the mountain."

"We will," Laurel said. "As soon as JoJo comes back with help."

"No," Mandy shook her head. "You have to take me now. I'm scared. He tried to kill me. If they bring him up while I'm still here, he'll try again. He's lost it. He blames you and Chris for getting captured by ISIS. His life went to hell because of it. He was glad Chris killed himself. Now, he wants me to die. Then he'll come for you. He's sick, I tell you.

Mandy stepped away from Laurel. "If you won't take me back, I'll go alone. I can't be here when they bring him up."

"We need to wait until JoJo comes back with

help," Laurel said. Rico wasn't there to go with her. He'd be mad if she left without him.

"You stay." Mandy turned and walked toward one of the four-wheelers.

Laurel ran after her. "You can't go down by yourself. The trails can be confusing. You could get lost."

"I'll risk it. I can't stay here." Mandy started to climb onto the four-wheeler.

"Fine," Laurel said. "I'll take you down in the ATV we came up in."

Mandy shook her head. "It's the biggest one out here. Won't they need it to bring Estep down?"

"Good point." Laurel glanced at the four-wheeler Mandy had been about to take. "I'll drive. You can hop on the back."

Laurel looked at the men standing at the edge of the cliff. No one was looking toward her and Mandy. She needed to let someone know they were going down the mountain.

Finally, one of the guys looked over his shoulder.

Laurel waved at him. "I'm taking Mandy down to the lodge," she called out. "Let Rico know."

The man nodded.

Laurel straddled the seat on the four-wheeler, started the engine and motioned for Mandy to get on the back.

The young widow slung her leg over the seat and scooted forward, wrapping her arms around Laurel's waist.

With one last glance toward the men working on rescuing Dr. Estep, Laurel gave the four-wheeler some gas and started down the trail.

She moved slowly, knowing if she went too fast, she might have trouble slowing their descent.

They'd gone about a third of the way down, and had just passed the entrance to the mine the mining company had expressed an interest in, when Mandy yelled, "Stop!"

Startled, Laurel hit the brakes hard, sending the four-wheeler skidding sideways.

When the ATV came to a stop, Laurel pressed a hand to her chest. Her heart was pounding hard against her ribs. "What's wrong?"

Mandy jumped off the back of the vehicle. "I can't," she said, her eyes wide and wild. "I can't go on like this. I lost my baby and now my husband. I have no one and nothing left to live for."

"Mandy," Laurel got off the four-wheeler. "You have your whole life ahead of you. Let me get you down to the lodge, and we can talk. You're not alone. You have me. I'll help you. I'd let you stay with me, but my apartment is too small. Gunny and RJ will let you stay at the lodge. You'll be surrounded by people who care. Please. Let me take you to the lodge."

The young woman shook her head. "I want to be with Chris and my baby. I have nothing left here." She spun and ran back up the trail.

"Mandy!" Laurel called out. She jumped back on the ATV, spun it around and raced after Mandy.

The woman had disappeared around a curve in the trail ahead of Laurel.

When Laurel drove around the corner, the trail opened up in front of the old mine.

Mandy ran through the entrance, disappearing into the darkness.

Laurel's heart leaped into her throat. "Mandy! Don't go in there." The old mines were death traps, with tunnels branching in all directions and some shafts that dropped straight down.

Laurel stopped the ATV in front of the mine and hopped off. Going in without a light source was dangerous. She lifted the seat on the ATV, looking for a stash of tools and maybe a flashlight. She'd about given up when she found a small keychain LED flashlight amongst a few tools.

Armed with the light, she entered the mine. "Mandy, sweetie, come outside in the light. Let's talk."

"I'm done," she called out, her voice echoing against the walls of the shaft.

"Chris would've wanted you to get on with your life."

"He didn't love me," Mandy said. "If he had, he wouldn't have left me alone."

The deeper she moved into the darkness, the faster Laurel's heart beat.

Sweet Jesus. Now was not the time for a panic attack.

"Mandy, come out into the light so we can talk."

"I'm done talking. Talking didn't save Chris from the demons that haunted him. He told me about the way they tortured him. He said they tortured him in front of you and Dr. Estep to get you and the doctor to tell them information about unit movements, secrets only you and the doctor knew."

"They tortured all three of us in front of each other," Laurel said, the memories her mind had suppressed surfacing. "We didn't have any secrets to tell."

"You're lying!" Mandy yelled. "If you'd told them what they'd wanted to know, they wouldn't have hurt him as badly as they did."

"Mandy, we were a medical team. They kidnapped us to save their leader. The man was too far gone to be saved. They tortured us because we let him die."

"Chris was supposed to come home to me," Mandy said. "We were supposed to start a family. He's dead, my baby's dead, and you and the doctor are living your best lives. It's not fair."

Laurel moved toward the sound of Mandy's voice. "Sometimes, life isn't fair, but you can't give up on it. There are so many reasons to live." Laurel shined her light in front of her, inching her way forward. She stopped when the floor of the tunnel ahead disappeared into a hole. A dark hole, much like the one she'd been shoved into in Syria.

Her heart leaped into her throat. She backed away, only to run into someone behind her.

"Why should you live when Chris is dead?" Mandy's voice sounded in her ear. "They hurt him to get you to talk. You and the doctor didn't say anything to make them stop."

Mandy stood between Laurel and her way out of the mine shaft.

"Nothing we could've said would've made them stop," Laurel said. "They were animals. We couldn't reason with them. They only wanted to see us writhe in pain."

"You could've said anything," Mandy said, her voice high-pitched. "You could've lied. Made up something. Anything to get them to stop."

"We did," Laurel said. "Nothing made them stop until the Navy SEALs got us out."

"Nothing matters anymore," Mandy said. "Chris is dead. I might as well be dead. We all have to die sometime."

The limited range of the keychain flashlight was enough light for Laurel to see the dead look in Mandy's eyes. She blamed Laurel and Dr. Estep for the severity of Chris's torture and subsequent suicide.

Laurel hadn't said anything to Mandy about the threats she'd received. Not the flag, the rose or the symbol on her car. Mandy knew she would deliver flowers to the church. She had to have been the one to lock her in the supply room.

Her husband's death and the loss of her baby had taken their toll on the young woman. She was hurting so badly she'd lost her grip on reality.

If Laurel could just get Mandy out of the mine and back to the lodge, she'd find the help the woman needed. "Mandy, come with me to the lodge. I'll make some hot cocoa. We'll sit together and talk."

"I'm done talking," Mandy said and shoved Laurel hard.

Laurel staggered backward and teetered on the edge of the down shaft. She reached out, her arms flailing until she latched onto Mandy.

Mandy screamed and pitched forward.

Still holding onto Mandy's arm, Laurel fell down the narrow, dark shaft, her last thought of Rico.

CHAPTER 14

WHEN RICO REACHED DR. ESTEP, the first thing he did was check the man for a pulse. When he found one, he let the others know the man was alive. Then he checked for broken bones and any lacerations that might cause the man to bleed out.

Nothing obvious surfaced.

The doctor stirred and moaned.

"Dr. Estep," Rico spoke to the man. "I need you to wake up. Dr. Estep."

Again, the man moaned. This time, his eyelids fluttered and opened, and he looked up into Rico's gaze.

"Where am I?" the doctor said.

"You fell over the ledge."

The doctor's eyes widened. "Mandy?

Rico shook his head. "Mrs. Monahan claims you tried to push her over the cliff."

Dr. Estep shook his head and winced. "No," he said, "she pushed me. She said something about blaming me and Laurel for Chris's death. Where is she? Where's Laurel?"

Rico's heart slammed into his belly. "Laurel was with Mandy."

Dr. Estep gripped Rico's arm. "Mandy isn't in her right mind. She blames me and Laurel for what happened to her husband. Laurel is in danger."

Rico was already on his feet. He raised his face and yelled. "Where's Laurel?"

One of the guys shouted back. "She took Monahan's wife down to the lodge."

"Bring me up!!" he yelled as he tied the rope around his middle.

Max leaned his head over the edge. "What?

"Bring me up. Now!" Rico yelled.

The rope around his middle tightened, drawing him upward. Rico glanced down at Dr. Estep. "Help is on the way."

"I'm not going anywhere," Estep said. "Go. Save Laurel."

Holding onto the rope, Rico scaled the side of the mountain. He pulled himself up over the edge, and his first words were, "Laurel's in trouble."

He ran for one of the four-wheelers.

Max ran after him. "Follow me, or you'll get lost.

The two men jumped onto the ATVs.

Max led the way down the mountain, going

slower than Rico would've liked but faster than was safe on the twisting, turning trails.

As he followed Max, Rico cursed himself for insisting on being the one to go down after Dr. Estep.

He'd left Laurel unprotected, trusting Mandy when she'd said Dr. Estep had tried to push her over the edge. Why hadn't he considered Mandy as the stalker?

Because she was the bereaved widow. Why would she want to hurt Laurel? Why would she blame Laurel and Dr. Estep for what had happened to her husband?

It didn't matter why. What mattered was Rico getting to Laurel before Mandy hurt her.

They picked up speed as the trail leveled out briefly and then slowed as they approached another turn.

They emerged into a clear area that ran in front of the old mine.

With his gaze on the trail and Max's four-wheeler in front of him, Rico almost missed seeing the four-wheeler parked at the entrance to the mine.

Rico slammed on his brakes and jerked the handlebars sideways, bringing the ATV to a skidding halt. Then he turned it around and punched the accelerator, sending the four-wheeler shooting toward the mine's entrance.

He came to a skidding halt next to the other four-wheeler, shifted his ATV into park and leaped off. "Laurel!" he yelled and ran into the mine.

After only a few steps, he realized he'd need a flashlight if he wanted to find something.

Rico ran out into the light and flipped the seat up on the ATV. He found a small flashlight among other tools and pressed the on button.

Nothing happened.

He slapped the flashlight in his palm. The light flickered on.

Rico raced into the old mine. "Laurel!"

All the while he ran, he berated himself. He shouldn't have left her.

"Laurel!" he shouted, the sound echoing off the shaft walls.

He was moving so fast he almost didn't see the hole in the floor until he was teetering on the edge. At the last moment, he leaned backward and sat. For a moment, he sucked in air, willing his heart and mind to slow so that he could think.

When he put his hands on the tunnel floor to push himself to his feet, he felt something cylindrical beneath his fingertips.

He shined his flashlight down on a keychain flashlight, and his stomach clenched.

Leaning over the edge of the hole, he focused the beam into what had to have been an air shaft for a tunnel far below. It wasn't wide enough to bring ore up in any significant amounts.

Twenty or more feet below was what appeared to be a tangle of arms, legs and hair jammed into that narrow shaft.

"Laurel?" he called out.

The twist of limbs moved slightly, and a moan sounded from below.

"Laurel, please answer me," he called out.

"Help me," another woman's voice cried. "I think my arm is broken. "Please. It hurts."

"Mandy?" A chill rippled down Rico's spine. "Where's Laurel?"

"She's...she's below me. She's not moving," Mandy said weakly.

Air lodged in Rico's lungs.

"She's dead," Mandy said.

Her words hit Rico like a giant fist slamming into his chest. "No," he whispered. She couldn't be.

Beautiful, smiling Laurel, who'd survived ISIS hell. Laurel, who'd come home to Fool's Gold, spreading happiness and warmth with the flowers she so dearly loved. Always smiling. Except when he'd told her they couldn't be together.

No. She wasn't dead. She couldn't be.

"Don't move," Rico said. "I'll get you out of there." And then he'd get Laurel out. She'd be all right. He just had to get to her.

He ran back to the four-wheeler parked outside the mine entrance. He didn't have ropes or carabiners he could use to rappel down into the shaft to bring the women up.

Desperate to find something, anything, he flipped the seat up on the four-wheeler and sifted through the tools and survival items. He found a small first-aid kit, zip ties, a hammer, some hook nails for fencing and an emergency survival blanket. He shoved zip ties into his back pocket and lifted the shiny emergency blanket. He shook it out and tested its length and strength. It wasn't long or strong enough to be used to climb down into the shaft.

He dug through the other items in the storage compartment, his hand sliding over a hand-held device that appeared to be a remote control. He pushed the button, and a motor whined. Rico followed the sound to the front of the four-wheeler and nearly collapsed in relief. A winch. Dear Lord, thank you for making Gunny and RJ smart enough to equip their ATVs with rescue equipment, including a remote-controlled winch.

He hoped the cable was long enough to reach all the way down to the women trapped in the shaft,

To improve the odds of the cable reaching, he had to get the four-wheeler closer to the shaft.

He pocketed the remote, climbed onto the four-wheeler and started the engine. As he eased through the entrance to the mine, he switched on the head-light and retraced the path through the different branches until he arrived several yards short of the air shaft.

"Still with me, Mandy?" he called out.

"Yes," she said. "Please, get me out of here."

Rico pulled several feet of cable out of the winch and frowned. It had a heavy-duty hook on the end, but that wouldn't help Mandy if she had a broken arm and couldn't hold onto it.

Tearing the shirt off his back, he twisted it into a thick, tight rope and tied both ends to the hook, forming a sling.

"I'm sending a cable down with a sling attached," he said. "Slip it over your head and under your arms. Let me know when you've done that, and I'll pull you out. Do you understand?"

"Yes," she replied.

Rico hit the remote control and lowered the sling and hook slowly down the shaft. He shined his flashlight, trying to gauge how much further it needed to go.

The winch stopped, having reached its maximum length.

"Can you reach the sling?" he called out.

A moment of silence stretched Rico's nerves.

"I have it," Mandy called out.

The cable swayed.

"I'm in the sling," Mandy said.

"Hold on. I'll bring you up." Rico hit the button on the remote. The winch rolled and tightened as it engaged Mandy's weight and brought her up the shaft.

As she neared the top, Rico slowed the ascent, stopping it when the sling and Mandy slid up and over the edge onto the floor of the mine shaft.

"Oh, thank God," Mandy breathed.

Rico helped her out of the sling and brought her to her feet. "Can you stand on your own?"

She nodded.

"What about your arm?" he asked.

She rolled her shoulder and flexed her elbow, wincing. "It's tender, but I can move it. Please, get me out of here."

"I have to get Laurel out first."

"She's dead," Mandy said. "There's nothing you can do for her."

"I'm bringing her out of the shaft." He walked toward Mandy, reaching into his back pocket for a zip tie. "Is there a reason you don't want me to bring her up?"

Mandy shook her head. "No."

As Rico neared her, Mandy backed away,

"Let me see your arm." Rico reached out his empty hand.

Mandy took another step backward, away from the glow of the four-wheeler's headlight. "It's fine. I need to get out of here into the sunshine."

"And so does Laurel. She doesn't like dark, tight places." Rico took another step toward Mandy. "But then you know that, don't you? Tight places like a church supply closet."

"I don't know what you're talking about," Mandy said. "You're scaring me."

"Give me your hand, Mandy," he said, his muscles tensing.

"No." She spun and ran into the darkness toward the mine's entrance.

Rico followed her to the mine entrance but stopped there as Mandy disappeared into the trees.

Laurel was still trapped in the shaft. He couldn't leave her to chase Mandy any further. The woman was on her own to get down the mountain.

Instead, he returned to the four-wheeler, slipped the sling over his shoulders and eased over the edge. Once he was dangling into the shaft, he slipped his hand into the pocket with the remote and pressed the button, lowering the winch and himself slowly down the shaft, shining the light below him.

"Laurel," he called out. "Sweetheart. Please, answer me."

He stopped short of her location, his feet dangling above her by mere inches. "Laurel." He held his breath, listening for any sound.

"Hey," she said, her voice barely above a whisper.

All the air left his lungs, and joy swelled in his heart.

Laurel was alive.

"Hey, yourself," he said softly.

"Is she gone?" Laurel murmured.

"She ran out of the mine."

"Don't trust her," Laurel said.

"I know. She's been the one behind your troubles. She pushed Dr. Estep over the edge."

"Is he okay?"

"He'll make it. Can you move at all?" he asked.

"I'm wedged in," she said. "I played dead so that Mandy wouldn't try to make me fall deeper."

Rico shined the flashlight around her body, passing the light over her face.

She looked up at him. "I'm afraid that if I move, I'll slip further down the shaft."

His heart lodged in his throat. The shaft could be another five, ten or a hundred feet deeper. He'd already reached the maximum length of the winch. She couldn't afford to fall further. "If I reach my hand down, could you take it?"

"Maybe," she said.

"I'm going to lower myself a little more so you don't have far to reach." He clipped the flashlight to the cable over his head to free his hands. Then he pulled his knees up, hit the remote button, and descended another six inches. The winch stopped on its own. It had extended to its maximum length.

"I'm going to reach down and try to touch you. Don't move yet."

"Okay," she said. "Have I told you lately that I don't like dark holes in the ground?"

He chuckled, though he didn't feel like it. Rico was terrified she'd move before he was ready and drop to the bottom, wherever that was.

"We're going to get out of this. We're a team, aren't we?"

"Uh-huh," she said. "I can see your hand. I think I can reach it."

"Don't," he said. "Let me get as close as possible where we can grab onto our wrists."

"Waiting," she responded.

Stretching as far as he could in the limited space he had to work with, he positioned his arm next to hers. "Let me do the work. Don't move your arm at all until I tell you to."

"Yes, sir," she said softly, her voice shaking.

He laid his arm next to hers and wrapped his fingers around her wrist. "Can you wrap your fingers around my wrist without moving your arm or shoulder?"

"I think so." Her fingers curled around his wrist.

"On three, I'm going to pull you up into my arms," he said. "Ready?"

"Ready," she said, her fingers tightening around his wrist.

Rico prayed he had enough strength and leverage to make it count. "One. Two."

He pulled hard. She was wedged in tightly, and for a moment, didn't budge. Then she shifted, her arm and shoulder coming up. When her body straightened, her feet fell down the shaft, jerking the rest of her downward.

Rico's grip slipped from around her wrist. She wasn't far enough up his body for him to grab her with his other hand.

Instead, he clamped her body between his legs, catching her before she plummeted the rest of the way down the shaft.

"Good catch," she said, wrapping her arms around his hips.

Rico's pulse pounded so hard against his eardrums he could barely hear himself think. He reached beneath her arms and pulled her up without fully releasing her from the leg lock.

When he had her wrapped securely in his arms, with her hands locked behind his neck, he breathed for the first time in what felt like a very long time. Rico buried his face against her neck for a long moment, shaking with the intensity of the fear that had gripped him.

"You have me," she said. "Let's get out of here."

He nodded and lowered one of his arms to fumble in his pocket for the winch remote. He pressed the button, sending them upward toward the light from the four-wheeler. Once they were moving, he dropped the remote in his pocket and wrapped his arms tightly around her, his legs circling hers. He wouldn't let go. Couldn't. She meant too much to him.

Laurel pressed a kiss against his cheek. "You're my hero, once again." She leaned back enough to look into his face. "I'm learning that life is too short not to take every opportunity to kiss the one you love."

"Agreed," he said and kissed her.

A loud bang sounded above them; fire flashed over the top of the shaft, and the cable they were suspended on jerked violently before the four-wheeler's headlight blinked out.

Rico and Laurel clung to each other as they dropped several inches before the cable steadied.

Steadied, as in, stayed perfectly still.

"What happened?" Laurel whispered.

"I don't know." Rico reached into his pocket for the remote and hit the up button.

Nothing.

Silence surrounded them.

Laurel chuckled. "Well, that was unexpected. What now?"

He didn't know. They were still a dozen or more feet from the top. If he was by himself, he might be able to brace his back against the side of the shaft and his feet on the opposite side to walk up to the top.

Laurel was too petite for that option to work for her.

"I swear I can hear your brain churning," Laurel said.

"Think you could crawl into this sling with me?" he asked.

She pushed her fingers between him and the fabric sling. "It would be a tight fit."

"If you can get into it, I can get out and crab-crawl between the walls of the shaft to the top."

"You won't fall, will you?" Laurel's arms tightened around his neck.

"No way. We're a team, remember. We're getting out of this together."

She nodded.

"I'll hold you with my legs and arms. You can let go of me and slip up between me and the V of the sling, which is being held by the winch hook."

"Okay." Laurel drew in a deep breath and dropped her hands from around his neck to his chest and then lower to slip between him and the sling.

Rico held onto her with all his strength. He could not fail.

Laurel got her arms into the sling, then ducked her head and pressed it against his chest. As she inched upward, her head made it through, and then her shoulders.

She had just folded her arms over the sling fabric when the cable jerked.

"What the hell?" Rico held onto Laurel as the cable vibrated, and then they were moving up the shaft.

"How's this happening?" Laurel said. "The remote wasn't working."

As realization dawned, Rico grinned. "The cavalry has arrived."

When they arrived at the top of the shaft and rolled out onto the ground, Rico stared up at the men crowded into the tunnel and grinned. "See?" he said. "The cavalry."

Jake Cogburn, Gunny, a man Rico had met named Levi Franks and Cage Weaver gathered around. Cage helped Laurel out of the sling and up onto her feet.

Once Rico untangled himself, Jake reached down to help him up.

"Great timing," Rico said.

"That's all RJ's doing," Jake said. "We were following JoJo up to the ridge when RJ spotted Mandy Monahan running out of the mine. She jumped out of the side-by-side and tackled her about the time the explosion went off in the mine."

Gunny chuckled. "My girl convinced Mrs. Monahan to talk. She said you'd gone down to bring Laurel up. Meanwhile, Mandy stuffed a shirt into the gas tank of the four-wheeler and set it on fire."

"We had to get the damaged four-wheeler out of the way before we could get to you and Laurel," Levi said. "So, we drove the other four-wheeler into the mine, hooked up its winch to the back of the damaged one and pulled it out of the way."

"We didn't realize we were reeling in the prized catch," Gunny said.

"Like I said," Rico laughed, "perfect timing."

"What happened to Mandy?" Laurel asked.

Jake grinned. "RJ's sitting on her."

Rico fished in his back pocket and handed Jake the zip ties. "These might help." He slipped his arm around Laurel's waist. "Now, if you don't mind, we could use a little sunshine."

Laurel leaned into him. They walked out of the mine into the sunshine.

Rico turned his face to the rays and breathed in the fresh mountain air.

Like Jake had said, RJ sat on Mandy, holding the widow's arm pinned behind her back between her shoulder blades.

Jake helped her secure the woman's wrists with a zip tie before they helped her to her feet.

Mandy glared at Laurel and muttered, "It's not fair."

Laurel met the woman's glare with a pitying glance. "Life's not fair. You have to get over it."

Jake led Mandy to a four-seater ATV, buckled her into the back seat and then sat beside her. RJ slipped into the driver's seat, and Gunny sat beside her.

"Are you going to be okay?" Devin asked Laurel.

She nodded. "I am now."

He tilted his head toward the mountain. "I'm going to go watch them evacuate the doctor."

At that moment, a helicopter flew overhead.

"Go," Laurel said. "I'm going to head down to the lodge. I've had enough excitement."

Devin and Levi mounted their four-wheelers and drove up the mountain.

"Do you want us to come back after we drop our guest off with the sheriff?" RJ asked.

Rico shook his head. "We'll take the good four-wheeler down."

RJ nodded. "See you at the lodge."

After everyone left, Rico pulled Laurel into his arms. "I almost lost you."

She wrapped her arms around his waist and leaned her cheek against his chest. "I almost lost you."

"We make a good team," Rico said.

"I know," she said, her arms tightening around him. "Doesn't make sense to break up something that works." She looked up into his eyes.

"I never want to hurt you," he said. "I'm broken."

"And I'm not?" She shook her head. "I say we stick together as a team and fix what's broken."

Rico stared at her jaw where the bruise was neatly covered by makeup. "I won't sleep with you until the nightmares stop."

"We'll work around that," she said, her smile spreading across her face.

He bent and claimed her lips in a kiss, his heart lighter than it had been since he'd left Syria with his friend in a body bag.

He knew it was because of Laurel, with her ready smile, her positive attitude and her kind and caring heart.

Hesitant to believe in fate, Rico had to think it was destiny that he'd been the one to bring Laurel out of Syria. They were meant to meet up again.

Whatever it was—fate, destiny or just dumb luck —he was happy it had happened to him.

EPILOGUE

ONE MONTH LATER...

RICO SAT in the swing on the porch of the Lost Valley Ranch lodge, with Laurel's head resting on his shoulder, completely content and happier than he'd been...ever.

Since Chris Monahan's memorial, Mandy Monahan had been committed to a mental hospital, where they would help her work through her depression and mania.

"Hey," Rico said, "what happened to Dr. Estep? I thought you invited him up for this barbeque."

"I did," she said. "He had a better offer."

"Did he?" Rico glanced down at her with raised eyebrows.

"He had a date with his next-door neighbor."

Laurel grinned. "She'd been bringing him meals and helping with a few chores around the house. Now that he's getting around a little better on crutches, she's been taking him on picnics. Tonight, they're at a concert in Denver."

"She drove, right?"

Laurel nodded.

"I'm happy for him." Rico pulled Laurel closer. "I'm happy for me."

"I'm happy your nightmares have disappeared," she said, snuggling closer.

"You two should get a room," Jake said from where he leaned against the porch rail, sipping a beer. He looked around at the men of his division and their significant others and smiled. "I have some good news."

The conversations died down, and everyone gave Jake their attention.

"I'm headed to West Yellowstone tomorrow. Hank's new Brotherhood Protectors Aviation Division is having its official launch with an infiltration exercise. Hank wanted me to come see what they can do."

"That's awesome," Tayo Perez said. "Will we get some use out of them?"

Rico grinned at Tayo's enthusiasm.

Tayo worked part-time at the Colorado Springs airport, teaching people how to jump out of planes with parachutes.

"That's the plan," Jake said. "We won't have to rely on the generosity of Hank's friends to fly us places anymore. And there will be helicopters to get us in and out of hostile situations."

"That could take us to a whole new level of services," Max Thornton said.

Jake gave a brief nod. "Count on it. We've got great teams here in Colorado, West Yellowstone and Eagle Rock. Hank just started another division in Louisiana called the Bayou Brotherhood, and I hear he's expanding operations in Hawaii."

Cage Weaver leaned close to his fiancée, Emily Strayhorn. "What do you think about transferring to Hawaii?"

Emily shook her head. "I wouldn't be opposed to a honeymoon there, but I love my Colorado Rockies, and my family and friends are here."

Jake's lips twisted in a crooked smile. "FYI. Hank doesn't need anyone to transfer from here to Hawaii. He's already started recruiting for the Hawaii and Bayou divisions."

"Damn," Cage muttered. "Guess I'll have to be satisfied with a honeymoon there."

"I could go on that honeymoon without you," Emily threatened.

"Not on your life." Cage pulled her into his arms.

Rico had met all the men in the Colorado division of the Brotherhood Protectors. They were good people and would do anything to help a teammate, just like they'd done on active duty.

He was proud to be a part of Hank Patterson's organization, where he could use his Navy SEAL training and skills to help others.

And he was especially proud Laurel Layne had run into him on a garden path and shown him how to be happy and live his best life with someone he loved.

In her eyes, he was her hero.

In his eyes, she'd saved him.

THE END

IF YOU'RE intrigued by Hank Patterson's new Brotherhood Protectors Aviation Division, check out the Team Eagle series in the Brotherhood Protectors World. These books were written by some of your favorite authors and feature characters and settings from my stories.

Brotherhood Protectors Yellowstone World
Team Eagle
Booker's Mission - Kris Norris
Hunter's Mission - Kendall Talbot

Gunn's Mission - Delilah Devlin
Xavier's Mission - Lori Matthews
Wyatt's Mission - Jen Talty

Bayou Brotherhood Protectors

Remy (#1)
Gerard (#2)
Lucas (#3)
Beau (#4)
Rafael (#5)
Valentin (#6)
Landry (#7)
Simon (#8)
Maurice (#9)
Jacques (#10)

REMY

BAYOU BROTHERHOOD PROTECTORS
BOOK #1

New York Times & USA Today
Bestselling Author

ELLE JAMES

REMY

New York Times & USA Today Bestselling Author

ELLE JAMES

CHAPTER 1

WITH THE SUN dipping over the treetops and dusk settling beneath the boughs of the cypress trees, Deputy Shelby Taylor checked her watch. It would be dark before long. She should be turning around and heading back to the town of Bayou Mambaloa.

Named after the bayou on the edge of which it perched, the town was Shelby's home, where she'd been born and raised. But for a seven-year break, she'd lived in that small town all of her life.

So many young people left Bayou Mambaloa as soon as they turned eighteen. Many went to college or left for employment in New Orleans, Baton Rouge, Houston or some other city. Good-paying jobs were scarce in Bayou Mambaloa unless you were a fishing guide or the owner of a bed and breakfast. The primary industries keeping the town alive were tourism and fishing.

Thankfully, between the two of them, there was enough work for the small town to thrive for at least nine months of the year. The three months of cooler weather gave the residents time to regroup, restock, paint and get ready for the busy part of the year.

As small as Bayou Mambaloa was, it had an inordinate amount of crime per capita. Thus necessitating a sheriff's department and sheriff's deputies, who worked the 911 dispatch calls, responding to everything from rogue alligators in residential pools to drug smuggling.

Shelby sighed. Having grown up on the bayou, she knew her way around on land and in the water.

Her father had always wanted a boy. When all her mother had produced was Shelby and her sister, he hadn't let that slow him down. A fishing guide, her father had taken her out fishing nearly three-hundred-and-sixty-five days of the year, allowing her to steer whatever watercraft he had at the time—pirogues, canoes, bass boats, Jon boats and even an airboat.

Whenever a call came needing someone to get out on the bayou, her name was first on the list. She had to admit that she preferred patrolling in a boat versus in one of the SUVs in the department's fleet. Still, there were so many tributaries, islands, twists and turns in the bayou that if smugglers hid there, they'd be hard to find, even for Shelby.

She'd been on the water since seven o'clock that

morning after an anonymous caller had reported seeing two men on an airboat offloading several wooden crates onto an island in the bayou.

The report came on the heels of a heads-up from a Narcotics Detective with the Louisiana State Police's Criminal Investigations Division.

An informant had said that a drug cartel had set up shop in or near Bayou Mambaloa. The parish Sheriff's Department was to report anything they might find that was suspicious or indicative of drug running in their area.

Because the tip had been anonymous, Sheriff Bergeron had sent Shelby out to investigate and report her findings. She was not to engage, just mark the spot with her GPS and get that information back as soon as possible.

The caller had given a general location, which could have included any number of islands.

Shelby had circled at least ten islands during the day, walked the length of half of them and found nothing.

The only time she'd returned to Marcelle's Marina had been to fill the boat's gas tank and grab a sandwich and more water. At that time, she'd checked in with Sheriff Bergeron. He hadn't had any more calls and hadn't heard from CID. With nothing pressing going on elsewhere in the parish, he'd had Shelby continue her search.

Normally, any chance to get out of the patrol car

and on the water was heaven for Shelby. Not that day. Oppressive, late summer heat bore down on her all day. With humidity at ninety-seven percent, she'd started sweating at eight in the morning, consumed a gallon of water and was completely drenched.

She wished it would go ahead and rain to wash away the stench of her perspiration. Maybe, in the process, the rain would lower the temperature to less than hell's fiery inferno.

She passed a weathered fishing shack and sighed as she read the fading sign painted in blue letters— The Later Gator Fishing Hut. She released the throttle and let the skiff float slowly by.

A rush of memories flooded through her, bringing a sad smile to her lips. Less than a month ago, she'd spent a stormy night in that shack with a man she'd harbored a school-girl crush on for over twenty years.

She'd insisted it would only be a one-night stand they'd both walk away from with no regrets. She didn't regret that night or making love to the man. It had been an amazing night, and the sex had been better than she'd ever dreamed it could be.

However, despite her reassurances to him, she'd come away with one regret.

It had only been one night.

She wanted more.

But that wasn't to be. He'd gone on to the job waiting for him in Montana, never looking back.

He'd left Bayou Mambaloa twenty years ago. His short visit hadn't been enough to bring him back for good.

She hadn't been enough to make him want to stay.

Shelby gave the motor a surge of gas, sending the skiff away from the hut, but her memories followed. Focusing on the waterway ahead, she tried to banish the man and the memories from her thoughts.

By the time she headed back to Marcelle's Marina, the heat had taken its toll. She was tired, cranky and not at her best.

Shelby almost missed the airboat parked in an inlet half-hidden among the drooping boughs of a cypress tree. If movement out of the corner of her eye hadn't caught her attention, she would have driven her boat past without noting the coordinates.

When she turned, she spotted two men climbing aboard an airboat filled with wooden crates.

At the same moment, the taller one of the two men spotted her, grabbed the other man's arm and pointed in her direction.

"Fuck," Shelby muttered and fumbled to capture the coordinates with her cell phone, knowing she wasn't supposed to engage. If these were truly drug smugglers, they would be heavily armed.

The tall man pulled a handgun out of his waistband, aimed at Shelby and fired.

As soon as the gun came out, Shelby ducked.

Though it missed her, the bullet hit the side of her boat.

She dropped her cell phone, hit the throttle and sent the skiff powering through the bayou as fast as the outboard motor would take her.

Another shot rang out over the sound of the engine. The bullet glanced off the top of the motor, cracking the casing, but the engine roared on.

Her heart pounding like a snare drum at a rock concert, Shelby sped through the water, spun around fields of tall marsh grass, hunkering low while hoping she would disappear from their sight long enough to lose herself in the bayou.

For a moment, she dared believe she'd succeeded as she skimmed past a long stretch of marsh grass. She raised her head to peer over the vegetation, looking back in the direction of the two men.

To her immediate right, bright headlights dispelled the dusky darkness as the airboat cleaved a path through the marsh grass, blasting toward her.

Her skiff, with its outboard motor, was no match for the other craft. She had to steer around marsh grass or risk getting her propeller tangled, which meant zig-zagging through the bayou to avoid vegetation.

Not the airboat. Instead of going around, it cut through the field of grass, barreling straight for Shelby in her skiff.

She spun the bow to the left, but not soon enough to avoid the collision.

The larger airboat rammed into the front of the small skiff. The force of the blow launched the skiff into the air.

Shelby was thrown into the water and sank into darkness to the silty floor of the bayou.

As she scrambled to get her bearings and struggled to swim to the surface, the skiff came down hard over her. If not for the water's surface breaking the boat's fall, it would have crushed her and broken her neck. Instead, the hard metal smacked her hard, sending her back down into the silt. Her lungs burned, and her vision blurred.

Her mind numbing, she had only one thought.

Air.

The black water of the bayou dragged at her clothing. The silt at her feet sucked her deeper.

Her head spun, and pain throbbed through her skull. She used every last ounce of strength and consciousness and pushed her booted feet into the silt, sending herself upward. As she surfaced, her head hit something hard, sending her back beneath the water before she could fill her lungs.

Shelby surfaced a second time, her cheek scraping the side of something as she breached the surface and sucked in a deep breath.

She blinked. Were her eyes even open? The darkness was so complete she wondered for a second if the blow making her head throb and her thoughts blur had blinded her. Or was this how it felt to be dead?

She raised her hand to touch the object that had scraped her cheek. Metal. In the back of her mind, she knew she was still in the boat, but it was upside-down. The metal in front of her was the bench she'd been seated on moments before. She wrapped her fingers around the bench to keep her head above water in the air pocket between the bottom of the boat and the bayou's surface.

A whirring sound moved away and then returned, growing louder the closer it came to the inverted skiff. It slowed as it approached. Then metal clanked against metal, and the skiff lurched, the bow dipping lower into the water.

Still holding onto the bench, Shelby's murky brain registered danger. She held on tightly to the bench as the skiff was pushed through the water.

The whir outside increased along with the sound of metal scraping on metal. The front end of the skiff dipped low in the water, dipping the hull lower. Soon, Shelby's head touched the bottom of the boat, and her nose barely cleared the surface.

Whatever was moving the skiff was forcing it deeper.

Shelby had to get out from beneath the boat or drown. Tipping her head back, she breathed in a last breath, released the bench and grabbed for the side of the skiff. She pulled herself toward the edge, ducked beneath it and swam as hard as she could, her efforts jerky, her clothes weighing her down. She couldn't see her hands in front of her, and her lungs screamed for air.

When she thought she couldn't go another inch further, her hands bumped into stalks. She wrapped her fingers around them and pulled herself between them, snaking her way into a forest of reeds. Once her feet bumped against them, she lifted her head above the water and sucked in air. For a moment, the darkness wasn't as dark; the thickening dusk and the glow of headlights gave her just enough light to make out the dark strands of marsh grass surrounding her.

The whirring sound was behind her. Metal-on-metal screeches pierced the air, moving toward her. The grass stalks bent, touching her feet.

In a burst of adrenaline, Shelby ducked beneath the water and threaded her way deeper into the marsh. She moved as fast as she could to get away from the looming hulk of the skiff, plowing toward her through the marsh, pushing the skiff beneath it.

The adrenaline and her strength waning, she barely stayed ahead of the skiff being bull-dozed through the grass.

Shelby surfaced for air, so tired she barely had the energy to breathe. It would be so much easier to die.

Holding onto several stalks, she turned to face her death.

The engine cut off. Two lights shined out over the marsh. Another light blinked to life, the beam sweeping over the skiff's hull and the surrounding area.

As the beam neared Shelby, she sank beneath the surface and shifted the reeds enough to cover her head. The beam shone across her position.

Shelby froze. For a long moment, the ray held steady. If it didn't move on soon, she'd be forced to surface to breathe.

When she thought her lungs would burst, the beam shifted past.

Shelby tilted her head back, let her nose and mouth rise to the surface and breathed in.

The light swept back her way so fast she didn't have time to duck lower. Shelby stiffened, her pulse pounding through her veins and throbbing in her head.

Before the light reached her, it snapped off.

She dared to raise her head out of the water enough to clear her ears.

"She has to be dead," a voice said.

Through the reeds, Shelby could just make out two silhouettes between the headlights of the airboat.

"We need to flip the skiff and make sure," a lower voice said.

"I'm not getting in that water to flip no skiff. I saw four alligators earlier."

"You don't see them now," the man with the lower voice argued.

"Exactly why I'm not getting in the water. You don't know where they are in the dark. If you want to check, you get in."

After a pause, the man with the deep voice said. "You're right. Alligators are sneaky bastards."

"Damn right," his partner agreed. "Besides, that woman's dead."

"And if she's not?"

The flashlight blinked on again, the beam directed at the skiff. "She'd better be," the guy with the higher voice said. "Do you see the lettering on the side of that boat?"

"S-h-e-r…" Low-voice man spoke each letter out loud and then paused.

"It spells sheriff," the other guy finished.

"Fuck," low-voice man swore. "We killed a goddamn sheriff?"

"Yeah." The flashlight blinked off. "Let's get the fuck out of here."

The airboat engine revved, and the huge fan on the back of the craft whirred to life. The airboat backed off the skiff and turned, the lights sweeping over Shelby's position.

She sank below the water's surface, the sound of the airboat rumbling in her ears.

Soon, the sound faded.

Shelby bobbed to the surface. The airboat was

gone, and with it, the bright lights. Clouds scudded across the night sky, alternately blocking and revealing a fingernail moon. When it wasn't shrouded in clouds, it glowed softly, turning the inky black into indigo blue.

Her strength waning and her vision fading in and out of a gray mist, Shelby couldn't think past the throbbing in her head.

Out of the haze, the man's comment about alligators surfaced.

She hadn't escaped death by drowning only to become dinner to a hungry reptile.

Somehow, she managed to push her way back through the marsh grass to the mangled hull of the skiff, now crushed low and only a couple of inches above the water's surface. Shelby tried to pull herself up onto the side of the slick metal hull. With nothing to grab hold of, she had no leverage, nor did she have the strength.

Swimming around to the stern, she stepped onto the motionless propeller. With her last ounce of strength and energy, she pushed upward and flopped her body onto the hull. Her forehead bounced against the metal, sending a sharp pain through her already aching head.

Though the clouds chose that moment to clear and let the moon shine down on the bayou, Shelby succumbed to darkness.

ABOUT THE AUTHOR

ELLE JAMES also writing as MYLA JACKSON is a *New York Times* and *USA Today* Bestselling author of books including cowboys, intrigues and paranormal adventures that keep her readers on the edges of their seats. When she's not at her computer, she's traveling, snow skiing, boating, or riding her ATV, dreaming up new stories. Learn more about Elle James at www.ellejames.com

Website | Facebook | Twitter | GoodReads | Newsletter | BookBub | Amazon

Or visit her alter ego Myla Jackson at
mylajackson.com
Website | Facebook | Twitter | Newsletter

Follow Me!
www.ellejames.com
ellejamesauthor@gmail.com

ALSO BY ELLE JAMES

Lucas (#3)

Beau (#4)

Rafael (#5)

Valentin (#6)

Landry (#7)

Simon (#8)

Maurice (#9)

Jacques (#10)

Brotherhood Protectors Yellowstone

Saving Kyla (#1)

Saving Chelsea (#2)

Saving Amanda (#3)

Saving Liliana (#4)

Saving Breely (#5)

Saving Savvie (#6)

Saving Jenna (#7)

Saving Peyton (#8)

Saving Londyn (#9)

Brotherhood Protectors Colorado

SEAL Salvation (#1)

Rocky Mountain Rescue (#2)

Ranger Redemption (#3)

Tactical Takeover (#4)

Dog Days of Christmas (#16)

Montana Rescue (#17)

Montana Ranger Returns (#18)

Brotherhood Protectors Boxed Set 1

Brotherhood Protectors Boxed Set 2

Brotherhood Protectors Boxed Set 3

Brotherhood Protectors Boxed Set 4

Brotherhood Protectors Boxed Set 5

Brotherhood Protectors Boxed Set 6

Iron Horse Legacy

Soldier's Duty (#1)

Ranger's Baby (#2)

Marine's Promise (#3)

SEAL's Vow (#4)

Warrior's Resolve (#5)

Drake (#6)

Grimm (#7)

Murdock (#8)

Utah (#9)

Judge (#10)

Delta Force Strong

Ivy's Delta (Delta Force 3 Crossover)

Breaking Silence (#1)

Breaking Rules (#2)

Breaking Away (#3)

Breaking Free (#4)

Breaking Hearts (#5)

Breaking Ties (#6)

Breaking Point (#7)

Breaking Dawn (#8)

Breaking Promises (#9)

Hearts & Heroes Series

Wyatt's War (#1)

Mack's Witness (#2)

Ronin's Return (#3)

Sam's Surrender (#4)

Hellfire Series

Hellfire, Texas (#1)

Justice Burning (#2)

Smoldering Desire (#3)

Hellfire in High Heels (#4)

Playing With Fire (#5)

Up in Flames (#6)

Total Meltdown (#7)

Take No Prisoners Series

The Billionaire Replacement Date (#8) coming soon

The Billionaire Wedding Date (#9) coming soon

Cajun Magic Mystery Series

Voodoo on the Bayou (#1)

Voodoo for Two (#2)

Deja Voodoo (#3)

Cajun Magic Mysteries Books 1-3

The Outriders

Homicide at Whiskey Gulch (#1)

Hideout at Whiskey Gulch (#2)

Held Hostage at Whiskey Gulch (#3)

Setup at Whiskey Gulch (#4)

Missing Witness at Whiskey Gulch (#5)

Cowboy Justice at Whiskey Gulch (#6)

Boys Behaving Badly Anthologies

Rogues (#1)

Blue Collar (#2)

Pirates (#3)

Stranded (#4)

First Responder (#5)

Silver Soldier's (#6)

Warrior's Conquest

Enslaved by the Viking Short Story

Conquests

Smokin' Hot Firemen

Protecting the Colton Bride

Protecting the Colton Bride & Colton's Cowboy Code

Heir to Murder

Secret Service Rescue

High Octane Heroes

Haunted

Engaged with the Boss

Cowboy Brigade

An Unexpected Clue

Under Suspicion, With Child

Texas-Size Secrets

Made in United States
Troutdale, OR
10/01/2024

23292644R00159